Yummy on a stick...

Loralei's mouth went dry when she saw the man from the docks. Tall and muscular. The kind of guy whose mere presence commanded attention.

Bringing her glass to her lips, she gulped down a huge swallow to relieve the pressure. It didn't quite work... Especially when she realized the blond surf god was heading straight for her.

Leaning down, he brushed his lips against hers, warm and soft.

Her mouth dropped open—she wasn't sure if the gesture was an invitation for him to kiss her again or because she knew she should say something, like *Who the hell are you?*

Before she could decide, his solid body was pressing against her, urging her to slide over into the corner of the booth. And she did. Which left her a little miffed and seriously bewild...

The heat of him seeped into ... em of her shorts had ridden u... ... and she could feel t... ...rs, smooth to hair-...

She found her ... ...ho are you?"

"Jack," he said, a... ... and brushing the single word ac... ...ensitive shell of her ear. Then he pulled ... and smiled down at her, managing to fill his expression with kindness, sensuality and predatory promise.

Oh, this guy was trouble. The kind of man who got whatever he wanted, whenever he wanted it...

Dear Reader,

I'm so excited to finally see the first of my SEALs of Fortune series in print. This is a project I've been working on for a very long time and it's so great to see the hard work come to life. *Under the Surface* kicks off the series pitting Jackson Duchane, part-owner in Trident Diving, against Loralei Lancaster, reluctant owner of Lancaster Diving and Salvage.

From their first meeting it's obvious that strong emotions seethe between these two. They cross swords time and again. And hunting for the same treasure doesn't help—especially when they both think the other is playing dirty. They might not like each other, but that doesn't stop them from wanting each other, and the passion between them burns too hot to resist!

Under the Surface is about looking beyond what you see and trusting your instincts...and your heart. I hope you enjoy Jackson and Loralei's story! And don't forget to come back to visit with the crew from Trident Diving in July with *Holding Her Breath*.

I'd love to hear from you at kirasinclair.com, or come chat with me on Twitter @kirasinclair.

Best wishes,

Kira

Kira Sinclair

—

Under the Surface

Recycling programs
for this product may
not exist in your area.

ISBN-13: 978-0-373-79840-7

Under the Surface

Copyright © 2015 by Kira Bazzel

Printed in U.S.A.

www.Harlequin.com

Kira Sinclair is an award-winning author who writes emotional, passionate contemporary romances. Double winner of the National Readers' Choice Award, her first foray into writing fiction was for a high school English assignment. Nothing could dampen her enthusiasm...not even being forced to read the love story aloud to the class. However, it definitely made her blush. Writing about striking, sexy heroes and passionate, determined women has always excited her. She lives with her two beautiful daughters in North Alabama. Kira loves to hear from readers at kirasinclair.com.

Books by Kira Sinclair

HARLEQUIN BLAZE

Whispers in the Dark

Afterburn

Caught Off Guard

What Might Have Been

Bring It On

Take It Down

Rub It In

The Risk-Taker

She's No Angel

The Devil She Knows

Captivate Me

Testing the Limits

Bring Me to Life

This book is dedicated to Tammy Henderson.
For sweating with me, challenging me to do more
and be better, listening to me vent, and being there
when I needed you most. I couldn't have gotten
through the last few months without you! Thanks
for being you...and for sharing my book obsession.

Prologue

THEY NEEDED MONEY. Desperately. But was it worth risking his life?

The moment Jackson Duchane had seen Lancaster Diving's battered, outdated equipment piled on the docks in Mobile, Alabama, that nasty sensation of impending doom had begun to crawl across his shoulders.

An oil company had hired the Lancaster team to blast away a thick layer of rock blocking access to a new line they wanted to drill in the Gulf. Easy enough. Or it should have been.

This was what he got for subcontracting to a diving company he'd never worked with before.

But Trident Diving couldn't afford to be picky right now. The company was new and business was slow. Opening Trident in his hometown of Jacksonville, Florida had been a dream years in the making for him and his partners Asher Reynolds and Knox McLemore. Their friendship had been forged in the heat of battle. All of them were ex-Navy SEALs. There was nothing quite like sharing miserable conditions or crawling through a hail of bullets together to make you appreciate someone else's strengths and how they shored up your weaknesses.

Jackson couldn't imagine being in business with anyone else. Including his sister, Kennedy, who ran the Trident offices while she finished college, the four of them made an awesome team.

He'd wanted to turn down this job, had even mentioned his concerns to Knox and Asher. There'd been something off about James Lancaster and his offer. Something Jackson hadn't been able to put his finger on. But Kennedy had quoted their pitiful bank balance to convince him.

He should have gone with his gut.

Now, a hundred feet below the surface of the water, it was too late to listen to instinct. And it was entirely possible that decision was going to cost him his damn life.

Where the hell had they found their explosives guy? And why wasn't anyone else freaking that he was setting the charges completely wrong?

Jesus Christ! Jackson was going to kill someone when they got back to the surface—assuming he lived that long.

Signaling frantically, he tried to get the attention of one of the other divers, but everyone was ignoring him. Typical. They'd been less than welcoming. Considering he'd stepped in at the last minute to replace someone, that had already pissed him off. James had made it sound as if the injured diver had been hurt on dry land, but Jackson was beginning to wonder.

The problem with the explosives wasn't the first safety violation he'd seen since coming aboard *Emily's Fortune*.

Screw it. He wasn't about to stick around and let himself or someone else get killed. He'd seen enough death and destruction during his years with the SEALs to last him a lifetime.

He, Knox and Asher could have handled the job, and a hell of a lot more efficiently. Not to mention safely.

And non-compete clause or not, after this he was going

to be talking to the client about what he'd seen and making a promise that his company could perform any future work better, safer and cheaper.

Streamlining his body, Jackson streaked toward the rocky outcropping where Brian, the explosives guy, was working and pushed him out of the way. Brian was propelled sideways several feet, enough for Jackson to take his place in front of the charges.

The response he got was expected, an angry glare and an answering shove. He ignored both. Within minutes he had the charges set correctly.

Wrapping a hand around Brian's arm, Jackson towed him back toward the surface, knowing they needed to get out of blast range. He gave the signal and everyone else on the team followed.

They rose up, blue sky slowly appearing above the waterline.

Jackson broke free, his body bursting up and then sinking back down. He spat the regulator out of his mouth, and was already yelling when the rest of the team surfaced beside him.

After climbing aboard the ship that bobbed several feet away, Jackson shed his equipment piece by piece, heading straight for James Lancaster, the owner and head of their team. He and James had gone a round or two already, so Jackson was fully prepared for this to become heated.

"What the hell happened down there, Duchane?"

"Damn hotshot SEAL thinks he knows every goddamn thing," Brian hollered from behind him.

Jackson balled his hands into fists in an attempt to keep them by his sides instead of planted in the asshole's face and growled, "Your idiot demo guy was about to blow every one of us to hell and back. He'd bypassed the trigger so the minute he set the charge it was going to blow."

He watched James' eyes widen. *Finally.*

"That's bullshit," Brian sputtered.

The other guys, who up to this point had been silent and watchful, muttered, shifting uncomfortably behind him.

"He just wanted to get his hands on some explosives," Brian continued.

Jackson took a single menacing step forward. He was quickly losing the slippery hold on his temper. But before he could act, James stepped between them, placing a heavy hand on his shoulder.

"Son," he started with a calming voice Jackson was so not in the mood to heed. "I think it would be better if we parted ways."

1

LORALEI LANCASTER FORCED back the lump of fear clogging her throat and walked out on the dock.

The damn thing moved beneath her feet, swaying with the gentle lap of the water. Only to her it felt like a tidal wave preparing to swamp her, sweep her over the side and down into the bright blue water.

For most people a trip to Turks and Caicos was a prime vacation. For her it was pure hell. She was surrounded by water. And not just standing out here on the dock. Every window she looked through seemed to have an ocean view.

Suck it up, buttercup.

She could hear her dad's voice, low and gruff in her head. It wasn't any more soothing now than it had been when he was alive. Not that she'd heard it very often.

In fact, growing up, she'd gone months without hearing from him at all. And seeing him…that had happened maybe once or twice a year, if she was lucky. Or maybe it had been lucky that he hadn't tried to drag her into the transient—and water-centric—life he'd led.

Maybe they both had been happier, although that didn't

quite negate Loralei's resentment. After her mother had died in a freak diving accident, her father had dumped her on the mainland and let his in-laws raise his daughter.

"Loralei!" Brian hollered from a ship that was tied several feet down the dock. To her it felt like a mile.

She'd taken barely a handful of steps onto the dock before her body had frozen. Now her feet refused to move. There weren't any railings for her to cling to for safety and support. Why weren't there railings to keep people from falling in to the water?

Some masochistic part of her brain urged her to look. To turn her head and glance down. But she didn't. She knew that would be too much.

Suddenly, Brian was standing in front of her, wrapping his arms around her stiff body. He didn't seem to notice that she was stuck. Which was good. Maybe no one would notice her fear of the water.

She'd worked so hard to keep the weakness a secret.

Logically, she knew it was silly. Hundreds of thousands of people got in the water each day and they didn't drown. But logic hadn't helped her over the years. The few times she'd attempted to dip her toe in a pool as a teenager hadn't gone well. And here she was, the brand-new owner of Lancaster Diving and Salvage. What the hell was she supposed to do with a diving company?

Especially one in such dire financial straits.

Loralei pulled up the same pep talk that had gotten her butt on the plane in Chicago. She just needed to get through the next few weeks. She could do this. She had to.

Her father, along with making her the sole beneficiary of a company she really didn't want, also had left her with the means to make the company profitable enough to at least be tempting to potential buyers. He had been hot on the trail of a legendary shipwreck, the *Chimera*.

History suggested the ship had sailed from the Virgin Islands toward New Orleans and the Confederate States to deliver supplies and munitions.

But many believed that hadn't been the only thing in the hold when a hurricane had set upon the ship and sunk it somewhere between Haiti and Turks and Caicos. According to legend, there was gold. Lots of it.

What Loralei had found historically interesting was that, if the rumors of gold were true, and if the ship had reached port as planned, the *Chimera*'s cargo could have changed the outcome of the war.

Of course, that was pure speculation. But a secret stash of gold provided by Caribbean plantation owners, who'd had a stake in the issues the Confederacy was fighting for...

As a historian, Loralei's interest had been piqued the moment she'd begun reading her father's research on the *Chimera*. But the story itself wasn't the only surprise. Until she'd found the documentation on the *Chimera*, she'd never known her father had been interested in history at all. She'd grown up thinking that her driving need to uncover the past and discover how people thought, loved, hated and lived had come out of nowhere.

Why had it taken her father's death to learn that they actually had something in common?

That, more than anything, haunted Loralei. And it was the biggest reason she'd pushed herself to come here, despite the damn water, and finish what he'd started.

According to the records she'd found, her dad had thought he'd narrowed down the potential resting places for the *Chimera*.

Finding the missing ship could make the difference between a debt-laden burden and a company that would be a nice boost to her bank account and allow her to focus on her academic and research career.

The problem was she couldn't afford to hire anyone to oversee the operation. She was already afraid she wouldn't be able to pay the divers' salaries. But she'd worry about that if and when it became a reality.

Brian wrapped an arm around her shoulders and propelled her forward.

Loralie almost told him thank you before she realized he wouldn't understand her meaning and bit back the words.

Her body was wooden, but at least it was heading in the right direction again.

She'd known this man most of her life, even if she could count on her hands and feet the number of times they'd actually been face-to-face. Brian had joined her dad's team when he was fifteen. It had been a logical jump from summers and holidays to working full time once he was out of high school.

When she was younger, Loralei could admit to being a little jealous at how much time her dad spent with this man instead of his own daughter. Now, she was just grateful to have someone who was knowledgeable about what was going on and could help her through the next few weeks.

Grasping her around the waist, Brian lifted her up the ladder and onto the deck of their ship, *Emily's Fortune.*

Seeing her mom's name painted along the side in peeling, faded red letters sent an unexpected jolt of pain through her chest.

Somehow she managed to push that down, too.

To her relief, Brian led her into the belly of the ship. She could still feel the gentle sway as waves rocked against the hull, but at least she didn't have to look at the water anymore. If she closed her eyes maybe she could convince herself she was on a train or a plane or something.

Although, the scent of salt in the air and the sound of sea birds pretty much killed that fantasy.

"The team from Trident is already here."

Dropping onto the bench running along the wall behind a table in the galley, Lorelei rubbed a hand over her temple. "What?"

"Trident. You know, the diving company I was telling you about over the phone."

"The one that's been stealing clients from us for the last eight months?"

"Yeah, that one. They're here."

Dropping her hand, Lorelei looked up at Brian. He was about nine years older than she was, although when he smiled he looked even older. All his time in the sea and sun had etched extra lines at the corners of his eyes and across his forehead. His skin was a deep, dark brown— a few shades darker than the natural caramel color she'd inherited from her Latin mother—and leathery.

"Why?"

Brian frowned, the line between his brows angling into a deep groove.

"I have no idea, but it makes me uneasy."

Yeah, it didn't exactly thrill her, either.

If Brian was telling her the truth—and she had no reason to doubt him—Trident had been a thorn in her dad's side for months.

It couldn't be coincidence that they'd shown up here now, could it?

No, her life didn't work that way.

"Damn, this means we have competition, doesn't it?"

"Probably."

JACKSON BLENDED INTO the bustling activity of the marina and watched.

He'd never seen the woman Brian greeted with a hug and a deep smile, but he supposed it wasn't a leap to assume she was Lancaster's daughter.

He'd heard James had died from a heart attack three months ago. Damn shame, but not surprising. He hadn't looked healthy the last time they'd spoken. Of course, the man had been red-faced and screaming at him.

It hadn't taken James long to realize Trident—and Jackson specifically—was poaching his clients. The man had made it damn easy to do. But James had been livid, storming into the Trident offices to throw his weight around and threaten him with that non-compete clause he'd originally signed.

By then Jackson had discovered just how much financial trouble Lancaster was in, so he'd told the man to go ahead and hire a lawyer—he'd known James couldn't afford one.

And he hadn't felt a single twinge of guilt. Not when people's lives and safety were involved.

That potential mishap with the explosives was how shit like oil rigs exploding and millions of gallons of crude spilling into pristine waters happened.

Several weeks later their front door had been smashed in and their offices ransacked. All the expensive dive equipment and computers had been left untouched, nothing of value missing.

It had taken Asher, Knox, Kennedy and himself several days to deal with the mess. There was no way to prove the burglars had paid an inordinate amount of attention to his research on the *Chimera*, or that the person behind the theft was James Lancaster, but his gut had told him that's what had happened.

He'd had plenty of experience trusting his gut. On dangerous missions those hunches often had been the difference between life and death.

And now his gut was telling him Lancaster Diving's presence in Turks and Caicos wasn't a coincidence. Loralei Lancaster disappeared below deck, Brian right behind her, his hand hovering at the small of her back without actually touching. The diving community was small and he'd made it his business to know everything he could about Lancaster Diving…including the woman who'd inherited the mess James had left behind.

Jackson almost felt sorry for her. But not enough to stop his campaign to put them out of business. Which was secondary to keeping them away from the *Chimera*. He'd been researching the shipwreck for the past ten years. There was no way he'd let the Lancaster team find her first. Especially using his own damn work.

There was no denying Loralei was beautiful. Exotic. Her skin was a deep, sun-kissed brown. The shorts she wore hugged the curves of her hips, leaving plenty of long, delicious leg on display. Her lightweight shirt fluttered loosely against her body, making her look tropical and carefree.

Based on the information he'd been able to gather, he'd expected her to be bold and unabashed as she'd walked across the dock toward *Emily's Fortune*. But she'd kept her gaze focused straight ahead, every movement of her body stiff.

Why?

He didn't know, and he didn't want to care. But the soldier in him couldn't help but catalogue and consider.

Part of him wanted to stomp down the dock, storm onto her ship and confront her.

But that wouldn't lead him anywhere. No doubt she'd

simply lie just as her father, Brian, and everyone else attached to Lancaster Diving had.

So, he had a better plan.

Crossing his arms over his chest, Jackson leaned against a low railing and settled in to wait. This was something he was comfortable with, trained to withstand the kind of boredom that could drive most men crazy.

He watched the ships coming and going from the marina so that anyone who noticed him would just assume he was a tourist taking in the native color. But he never lost sight of Lancaster's ship.

Luckily, his wait wasn't very long. An hour later Loralei emerged, Brian still glued to her side.

She kept her head high and her focus squarely in front of her. Brian's mouth moved, but Jackson couldn't hear what the man said. Not that it particularly mattered. Loralei was either bored or unimpressed because she didn't bother responding. Her mouth was pulled into a tight line and her body strung with tension.

Her long black hair swirled in the soft breeze blowing off the water. For some reason he'd expected her eyes to be deep brown, but as she drew nearer Jackson realized they were actually a pale green. Like her father's.

It was about the only resemblance he found between the bear of a man with red-tinged skin permanently burned from too many years in the sun and harsh sea air, and the woman striding ever closer.

Jackson didn't bother moving as they drew even. Both of them were absorbed. Brian didn't notice him at all.

Loralei's gaze, though, brushed over him. And lingered. Not on his face, but on his body. He knew what she saw. He'd spent years honing his form into the weapon he needed it to be. He depended on strength and mobility to get the job done.

He was used to women noticing him. And he had to admit, the danger and secrecy of being a SEAL helped build a reputation many women found appealing. Over the years Jackson had been happy to take advantage of that job perk.

It had been months since he'd had the time to indulge, though. All his focus and energy had been going into opening Trident, building a reputation and client list, and gathering the research and capital to fund this search for the *Chimera*.

It irritated him that Loralei Lancaster stirred to life the first hint of awareness he'd felt in eighteen months.

Apparently, his dick didn't feel like being picky. Good thing his brain had better sense.

Her perusal only lasted a few moments, enough time for her to walk past him and then it was gone. But the sensation she'd awakened lingered, an unwanted buzz beneath his skin.

Clamping his fingers around the railing, Jackson forced himself not to turn and watch her walk away. There was no point. He knew exactly where to find her.

LORALEI NEEDED A DRINK. Or several. Yep, definitely several of those pretty orange and pink things every restaurant and bar seemed to offer. Fruity concoctions with enough alcohol to help her forget that tomorrow she would be on a ship surrounded by nothing but ocean.

God, she wished Melody was here. Her best friend had offered to come, but she couldn't get the time off. Melody was about the only person who knew of Loralei's phobia. She supposed it wasn't that important to keep it a secret, but she didn't like weakness—especially in herself. And it was difficult to look at her fear as anything but that. Over the years she'd tried to logic herself out of the irrational reaction, but nothing seemed to work.

Melody had discovered the truth by accident several years into their friendship. Even then, Loralei had been reluctant to admit the extent of her phobia until her friend had backed her into a corner, unwilling to accept her lies.

She didn't bother changing clothes before heading down to the bar attached to the hotel. She wasn't in the market to get picked up so she didn't care if her makeup was smudged and her clothes wrinkled after a long day of traveling.

She honestly didn't care about anything aside from settling her nerves.

Walking across the plush carpet, she let the dim light and soft sounds wash over her. If not for the calypso music and beach-chic decor, she might have been able to convince herself she was home in Chicago, which is where she'd much rather be, instead of on a Caribbean island.

Sliding into a booth in the far corner, she placed her order and then drilled her fingers into the table while she waited for it to be delivered. She should probably order food, too, but she didn't. Maybe in a bit, when her stomach stopped churning.

Her waitress dropped a heavy margarita glass onto a tiny white napkin and then slipped away. Loralei brought the drink to her lips and sipped, closing her eyes in pleasure as the fruity taste of it exploded across her tongue. Pineapple, strawberries, possibly mango.

When she opened her eyes again a man stood at the end of her table watching her. She started. The slushy contents of her glass rocked over the edge, sliding thickly down the angled curve to pool on her fingers.

With a frown, Loralei switched hands, brought her fingers to her mouth and sucked.

The man groaned low in his throat. Uneasiness crawled up to settle right between her shoulder blades.

"Do you mind if I sit?" he asked, folding his body in half before he'd finished the question.

"Yes, I do mind. Nothing personal, but I'm not looking for company."

His body stalled, shock crossing his face for the briefest moment before it was gone again. She supposed he was the kind of guy who didn't hear the word *no* often. He was handsome enough in a professional kind of way. Probably on vacation. Possibly with a wife upstairs.

A smarmy smile replaced his startled expression, as if he expected she would change her mind at any moment.

Something about this guy made her seriously uncomfortable. And that was saying something considering the emotional turmoil she'd already been struggling with.

At least he straightened, keeping his rear from occupying the seat opposite her. "Let me buy you another drink."

"Nope, I just got this one and I plan on nursing it for a while."

She hadn't been, but what was a little white lie in the grand scheme of things? Nothing if it kept his guy away from her.

Out of the corner of her eye, Loralei watched a man she'd noticed on the docks stalk across the bar. Over her admirer's shoulder, she saw him walking in their direction.

Now *he* was gorgeous in a blond-surf-god kind of way. Tall, if she had to guess, several inches over six feet. Being five-ten she was used to looking most men in the eye. But not him.

If she'd been here to pick up someone, he definitely would have been on her list of prospects. Tall and muscular. The kind of guy whose mere presence commanded attention.

Yummy on a stick, as Melody would say.

He was wearing a pair of khaki shorts with about a million pockets sewn up and down the thighs. A pale blue polo stretched taut across his broad chest, the soft material doing little to conceal the swell of pecks and dip of abs. He hadn't bothered to fasten the three tiny buttons, and she could see a dusting of pale blond hair that swept across his chest.

The color perfectly matched the honey-toned, tousled hair on his head, which looked as if he, the wind or some red-lipped siren had just been ruffling through it.

Loralei's mouth went dry. Bringing the glass she still held to her lips, she gulped down a huge swallow of the slushy goodness to try to relieve the pressure. It didn't quite work.

Especially when she realized the bronzed god was heading straight for her and not to one of the nearby tables.

She barely had time for a full breath before he was pushing the guy she'd completely forgotten out of the way.

"Excuse me," he said, drawing close to her.

Leaning down, he brushed his mouth against hers, warm and soft. All Loralei could do was sit there and stare up at him.

"Sorry I'm late, baby," he murmured, the low timber of his voice making every muscle in her body melt. She was pretty sure he'd also liquefied the frozen drink in her glass.

Somehow she managed to murmur something that obviously passed as appropriate because he smiled down at her, his unbelievably blue eyes twinkling with mirth and mischief.

Loralei's mouth dropped open—she wasn't sure if the gesture was an invitation for him to kiss her again or because she knew she should say something like, *Who the hell are you?*

Before she could decide, his solid body was pressing against her, urging her to slide over into the corner of the booth.

And she did, which left her a little miffed and seriously bewildered.

The guy still standing at the end of the table sputtered. "I thought you weren't looking for company."

"She isn't. She already has me."

The guy frowned. Anger flared deep in his eyes. "Why didn't you tell me you were here with someone?"

Because she wasn't. Although, she was coherent enough to realize it wouldn't be smart to say that out loud right now. So, she simply offered a shrug and an apologetic half smile.

With a labored huff, the guy finally walked away, apparently realizing arguing with her wasn't going to get him anywhere. Especially with the wall of masculinity sitting between them. The guy would have been mental to take on the man currently pressed against her body from shoulder to hip.

The heat of him seeped into her flesh. Maybe she should have changed clothes, put on longer shorts. The hem had ridden up her thigh at some point and she could feel the rub of his skin against hers, smooth to hair-roughened.

She found her voice enough to ask, "Who are you?" She kept the words pitched low so only he could hear them.

Draping an arm across the back of the booth, he squeezed in closer. A few seconds ago she would have thought that physically impossible. She was obviously wrong.

"Jack," he said, dipping his head and brushing the single word across the sensitive shell of her ear.

"Nice to meet you," she answered without thought or intent.

Pulling back, he smiled down at her. A shiver snaked through her stomach. Somehow he managed to fill his expression with kindness, sensuality and predatory promise. Apparently a deadly combination to her libido.

Loralei shifted in her seat. "What are you doing here?"

He shrugged, his entire ribcage lifting and sliding against her. "Rescuing you. I would have thought that was obvious."

"Well, yes, but why?"

His smile changed, going a little dangerous around the edges. "Because I wanted to."

Oh, this guy was trouble. Clearly. The kind of man who got whatever he wanted, whenever he wanted it.

Too bad. Tonight he was going to be disappointed, because he couldn't have her.

2

JACKSON WATCHED LORALEI LANCASTER'S eyes narrow. Part of him wanted to laugh. The rest wanted to pull her harder against his body.

From a distance she was beautiful. Up close…she was gorgeous. Even in the low bar light, her skin was luminous. Like sunlight filtering through the bright blue surface of the water in the last few moments of a great dive.

He had the same sensation sitting next to her that he'd felt when he'd finally narrowed down the *Chimera*'s location: reverence, triumph, pleasure.

He wasn't supposed to feel anything but anger and a desire for retribution around her.

Reminding himself of his reason for coming in the bar after her tonight, Jackson tried to fight temptation. It didn't help much since he could still feel her smooth, warm skin pressed against his thigh.

"I'll tell you the same thing I told him," she began, tilting her head toward the guy who'd already moved on to his next target across the bar. "I'm not interested."

"Hmm," he purred low in his throat. Some imp inside urged him to prove the lie in her words. He'd felt her response to the kiss he'd given her. And if he was honest, he wanted to feel it again.

Dipping his head, he breathed deep, pulling the sweet vanilla scent of her into his lungs. And then he brushed his mouth across hers.

She gasped, but she didn't pull away. Instead, her entire body swayed toward him.

He couldn't ignore the unexpected invitation. Even if he'd only meant to prove a point. Licking across her parted lips, he dipped inside. She tasted even sweeter than she smelled.

Moving his palm to the back of her neck, he cupped her head and brought her closer. A strangled sound vibrated from her throat.

Slowly, Jackson pulled away, relishing the glazed expression in her striking eyes.

"You sure about that?" he breathed into her ear.

She stared up at him, the far-away glimmer disappearing only to be replaced with a sharp glint that had the blood in his veins whooshing faster. Her mouth pulled into the hard curve of a frown. And Jackson braced for the backlash he knew was coming, even with his fingers still tangled in the soft strands of her hair.

Loralei reached for the glass sitting on the table in front of her. It didn't take a genius to see where this was headed, but he did nothing to actually stop her. Would she go through with it?

Tipping the glass, she let the cold, half-melted contents slide out over his head.

Apparently, she would.

Her pale green eyes flashed with fire. Air gushed in and out of her lungs, forcing her breasts tight against the thin barrier of her shirt.

God, could she get any more beautiful?

Or treacherous?

That's what he had to remember, though his body was begging him to give her another outlet for all that pent-up passion. He couldn't trust her. Or anyone attached to Lancaster.

Jackson didn't move, not even to wipe away the sunset-colored concoction sliding over his ears, into his collar and down the back of his neck.

He grinned at her, a cocky half smile that only made her growl long and low.

"Let me go."

"Not until we discuss why you're on this island, Loralei."

She stilled, her entire body going taut with attention. "I didn't tell you my name."

"No, you didn't."

"So how do you know it?"

"I know a lot of things, including what you're here to search for. Let me promise that you won't find the *Chimera*. You can't. Your dad didn't manage to steal enough information to actually find the wreckage. You're going to waste time and money, and my team will get there first."

She blinked up at him, but it wasn't a deer-in-the-headlights expression. Nope, she was thinking. The wheels in her brain moving at lightning speed. It was intoxicating to watch.

He'd always been drawn to intelligent women. He wanted more than a beautiful face and rocking body. He needed someone who could challenge him. Thrill him.

Which was why he stuck to inviting the uncomplicated ones to his bed. No fear of getting attached with them. Until recently, his life hadn't been conducive to long-term anything. Hell, he'd barely been willing to sign more than a one-month lease. He never knew how long he'd be in any one place, especially when assignments could last months at a time.

Since joining the Navy at eighteen, the past year and a half had been one of the longest stretches he'd spent in one place. And he'd been too damn busy to think about anything aside from a quick release of tension.

If Loralei Lancaster hadn't been part of the team that had stolen his research, both his body and brain definitely would be interested. So maybe it was better they were adversaries. He didn't need any distractions right now.

"Trident," was the first word she uttered.

"Brilliant deduction, baby."

"Don't call me baby."

Jackson shrugged.

"Which one of the assholes are you?"

"Assholes?" He took offense at that. Especially considering she was the one throwing the term around so blithely.

"Assholes, owners—same difference."

Jackson laughed bitterly. "I hardly think so, princess. Ask your good friend Brian all about assholes. He came about thirty seconds away from blowing me and everyone else on your father's team sky high eight months ago."

"I don't believe you."

"Suit yourself. Either way, you're wasting your time here in paradise. Go back home to Chicago where you belong."

Her arms crossed over her chest, Loralei glared at him. "If that was true you wouldn't be bothering to tell me. You'd just laugh at me from the deck of your ship like the world-class prick you are. What do you have against me?"

"You personally? Nothing." Yet. "But your dad and his crew? Plenty. They nearly got me killed, fired me and then stole from me."

"They stole from *you*? According to Brian you've been stealing our clients for months."

"It isn't stealing, princess, if they want to leave. And I promise, taking them was so damn easy. I didn't even have to undercut your price by very much. Most of the clients were more impressed with our professional, experienced and safety-conscious company."

Her mouth worked for several moments, no doubt holding back the stream of words she wanted to fling at him. He had to give her credit for controlling her reaction.

"But let's go back to the stealing issue. Where do you think your father got his research on the *Chimera*? I can promise you it wasn't by spending every spare moment over the last decade tracking ocean currents, researching historical records and meticulously plotting out potential courses for the ship."

Loralei shook her head. He could see the denial clouding her eyes. She didn't want to believe what he was saying, not about her father.

He understood. There was a time in his life, long ago, when he hadn't wanted to believe his own mother was capable of abandoning him without a second thought or glance back.

Sometimes reality wasn't fun. That didn't make it any less true. And everyone had to learn to deal with the dirty truth. He certainly had. Loralei would survive learning that her old man wasn't who she thought he'd been.

Or she'd reveal that she was just like him.

Either way, he'd at least know where he stood with Lancaster Diving and could plan his next move accordingly.

"Leave," she said finally, her lips barely moving on the low, menacing word.

Pushing slowly out of the booth, Jackson did as she'd asked. He watched her take a deep, calming breath as the space between them grew. He understood the instinct, felt the urge to clear her from his own lungs so that he could think again.

Instead, he stood at the end of her table and stared down at her.

"Think about what I said, Loralei. Your dad didn't get all my research, so the chances are you won't be looking in the right location. You're wasting time and money. And if my information is correct, you can't afford either right now."

LORALEI WATCHED THE brute of a man walk away from her. Her mind spun drunkenly, as if she'd had several of those damn drinks instead of a few measly sips before wasting good alcohol to soak his head.

She assumed Jack was short for Jackson Duchane, one of the owners of Trident. Brian had told her something about each of them. If she'd been paying attention and not trying to drown her neuroses in alcohol she might have clued in to who he was before giving him the chance to humiliate her.

Just remembering the way her body had reacted to him sent a wave of embarrassment across her skin. Great. Just what she needed.

The things he'd said about her dad… They'd hurt.

Could they be true? She'd always thought of her father as a big, distant, honorable guy. On the few occasions he'd come inland and spent time with her, he'd always admonished her to be a good girl. A good person. Stay away from drugs. Don't let boys pressure you into doing anything stupid. Follow the Ten Commandments. Listen to your grandparents.

What part of those rules allowed him to steal from Jackson Duchane and his partners?

None of them.

But she was old enough to realize parents sometimes said one thing and did another. She'd just never gotten that impression with her own father. Not that he'd been around enough for her to really know.

And that was the damn kicker.

She couldn't look Jackson in the eye and call him a liar because she didn't *know*.

Her gut told her it was possible. Lancaster Diving was in serious financial trouble. And, according to Brian, her dad had blamed Trident for that situation. If that was the case, would he have felt justified in bending the rules?

Possibly. Probably.

Damn it!

So, what the hell was she going to do? She'd put all of her eggs in this one basket. This salvage was her salvation. *Their* salvation. All the guys who'd spent their lives following her father around the world, taking jobs wherever they had to in order to make a living.

She couldn't ask Brian if what Jackson said was true. He'd probably just lie to her.

Or maybe it wouldn't be a lie.

If her father had stolen from them, why hadn't Trident pressed charges?

Because they couldn't prove it.

Sitting there alone in the booth, Loralei came to a stunning realization. The asshole was playing mind games. He knew they were after the same treasure, and he was trying to cut her off at the pass. Convince her to walk away before the fight had started.

What irked her even more was that he'd used his beautiful body, dangerous charm and sex appeal to do it. He hadn't hesitated to crowd into her personal space, kiss the hell out of her and get her all flustered before dropping his verbal bomb.

Dirty, nasty fighting.

And she'd fallen for it.

But she wouldn't again. Nope. Next time she'd be prepared for Jackson Duchane. Maybe she'd turn the tables, give him a dose of his own medicine.

She smiled gleefully. This was going to be fun.

More fun than she'd ever expected when she'd boarded the plane for a damn island.

JESUS, MARY AND JOSEPH, what had she been thinking?

Loralei crept across the deck of Jackson Duchane's ship. She hadn't intended to board the ship when she'd come to the marina but…

Honestly, she had no idea what she'd intended. Opportunity had presented itself. She'd been watching the ship, trying to get a feel for Jackson's setup and crew. One thing was for sure, his equipment was better than theirs.

Loralei tamped down a brief spurt of jealousy mixed with anger. Of course his equipment was better. He was taking all of their work and money.

As she'd loitered, the entire crew had left the ship. She wasn't certain where they were going at twenty minutes before midnight, but she honestly didn't care.

The ship was empty.

And it was a chance she couldn't pass up.

So she was standing on Jackson's ship, the deck rolling beneath her feet as she attempted to gain control of the panic welling up in her chest.

Deep breath in. Deep breath out.

Loralei pulled her gaze from the water. Her legs were stiff, knees refusing to bend as she shuffled toward the doorway that led down into even more darkness.

But at least she was inside.

The ship was huge, much bigger than hers. *Amphitrite* had been painted along the side in bold, curling letters. The boat clearly had been named for the Greek goddess of the sea and wife of Poseidon. She was definitely more modern, though, with a high-tech bridge and sonar system.

Since Loralei didn't know enough about either, she steered clear of both, creeping farther down the darkened hallway. She passed several closed doors, paused to open a few. They appeared to be sleeping berths. The last room opened to an office of sorts.

Papers were spread across a large table that was bolted to the floor. Moving forward, Loralei sifted through them. It took her several moments to realize they were maps of islands. Not Turks and Caicos, but possibly the smaller islands dotting the water around?

She flipped through several, unsure what she was looking at. For the first time, she wished she'd paid more attention when her dad had tried to teach her about some of this stuff. But considering her phobia, it had seemed a waste of time.

And Loralei hated wasting time.

The small room was too dark for her to make out the tiny lettering. And she didn't want to risk turning on a light and catching someone's attention.

Grabbing a handful, she moved toward the porthole cut high on the wall. Moonlight filtered through, giving her something to see by.

Holding the papers higher, she read the name of an inlet that she recognized. Her crew was heading there first thing in the morning. There was some speculation that the *Chimera* had sought shelter there before the storm hit. But, according to statements gathered from another ship that had been close, the ship's anchors had snapped in the high winds and it had been dragged out to open sea.

Which made the inlet a good place to start.

Apparently, Jackson Duchane had the same intention.

Unease and guilt crept up Loralei's spine. What was she doing? She shouldn't be here. This felt wrong.

Dropping the papers back on the table, she tried to remember how they'd been arranged. Probably something she should have paid attention to before touching them. Dammit, she couldn't even break and enter without screwing up something.

Above her, a sound rang through the ship.

Loralei instinctively dropped into a crouch.

Gripping the edge of a chair, she shook her head. Probably just some rigging clanging with the sway of the ship. No one was onboard. But her frantic heartbeat urged her to go. Deciding to listen, Loralei cracked open the door and slipped back into the dark hallway.

The doorway was three feet away when she heard the low murmur of a voice.

"No, having you and Knox here wouldn't be helpful just yet. Let me and the crew handle the preliminary dives. We need you on the Prescott job right now, and someone has to stay at the office to run things."

Loralei froze. Even the breath in her lungs stilled. A shadow drifted across a rectangle of light in the hallway a few feet away. Every muscle in her body tensed to fight or run, but the shadow passed. The low murmur of Jackson's voice faded and her lungs released the breath she'd been holding in a shaky stream.

It would not look good for Jackson to find her here right now. Maybe she should have thought of that before creeping on board.

Based on his shadow and sound, Jackson had gone left.

So it should be safe for her to go right, which was also the fastest route off this rocking torture chamber.

Loralei carefully poked her head out and swept her gaze across what little of the ship she could see. The coast appeared to be clear. It was now or never.

She kept low and stuck to the shadows as much as possible. She was out of the hold and nearly home free when her shoulder collided with something. A metallic clank echoed into the night.

Her stomach rolled. The ship pitched. She stared at the midnight blue expanse of water spread out beneath her.

Bile rose into her throat, burning a path and stinging her nose.

God, she was going to throw up.

3

"WHAT THE HELL was that?"

Jackson spun on his heel and looked toward the stern.

"What was what?" Asher asked in his ear.

"I have to call you back. I think someone's on the ship."

"God, I hope so, Jack. We have several crew."

"I sent them in to town for a last hurrah before I crack the whip."

"So, one of the guys struck out and came back early."

"Maybe." But something was off. Jackson's senses were tingling. He hadn't heard anyone approach.

"You're not in a war zone anymore, man. Time to let that shit go."

He wanted to argue the point, but Jackson had bigger things to deal with, so let his friend's comment slide.

Asher might be a prick on occasion, but there was no one Jackson would rather have at his back in a shit storm. They'd been assigned to the same platoon when he'd first come out of BUD/S training with the SEALs. Asher had taken a bullet for him. That was a debt not easily or quickly repaid.

"Whatever. I'll check in tomorrow." Jackson didn't

bother saying goodbye before ending the call and pocketing his cell.

He was already striding across the deck on feet that didn't make a single sound. His body was tense, prepared for whatever might spring out at him.

What he wasn't prepared for was finding Loralei Lancaster crouched down beside the railing, her fingers gripping the metal so hard the veins across the back of her hands threatened to pop through the skin.

He shouldn't be surprised, but he was.

Arms crossed over his chest, Jackson changed his stride, no longer concerned with concealing his approach. The soles of his shoes squeaked across the deck, but she didn't flinch. Her gaze, trained on the water, never wavered.

"What the hell do you think you're doing?"

She didn't respond.

Her breath was quick and shallow, probably a reaction to being caught in the act.

Reaching down, he grasped her arms and hauled her up. Her fingers released the railing and clamped on him, digging into his chest. Finally, she looked up at him. Shadows melted across her face, shielding her eyes and preventing him from reading her expression.

"Why are you on my ship, Loralei?"

She shook her head, moving it back and forth as if in slow motion.

"Hoping to get your hands on the information your daddy missed? Well, too bad, princess. I've been more careful in the last few months. There's nothing useful for you to find."

A spark kindled in her eyes. He watched her chest rise

and hold on a deep breath that she finally released with a whoosh of words. "Let me go."

"Why should I do that? I think contacting the authorities is a better option."

Her spine snapped straight. "And tell them what? You found me on the deck of your ship? I came here looking for you so I could talk. Clear up whatever misunderstanding you're laboring beneath."

He scoffed. "Why were you huddled in the shadows, then? Sell the lie to someone who might believe it."

Her gaze slipped sideways before quickly jerking back to his. "I dropped something."

"What? The hammer you were hoping to brain me with? Or maybe you're a knife kind of girl, look straight into someone's eyes as you slip the blade between their ribs."

She gasped, her eyes going wide before narrowing down to slits.

"What the hell are you talking about? I have no desire to hurt you."

"Sure, that's what they all say. I've seen plenty of blood-thirsty people in my life—women included—perfectly capable of killing with whatever was handy. Bomb, gun, bare hands. When you've watched a ten-year-old boy blow himself up because someone told him to, you learn not to underestimate anyone's capacity to cause physical harm."

She blinked at him, her mouth going slack for several moments.

"That's...awful."

"Tell me about it."

Her fingers, which were still dug deep into his chest, uncurled, but she didn't remove them. Instead, she spread them wide, pressing the warmth of her palm hard against him.

"I'm sorry." Her words were soft. For the briefest moment, he wanted to believe them.

And then he remembered who she was and why she was standing on the deck of his ship.

The anger he'd been suppressing for months—ever since realizing her father had broken in and stolen his work—roared to life.

Bending, he swept her into his arms.

She was lighter than she looked. Not that she appeared heavy, but she was tall.

"What are you doing?"

"Providing you a quick exit. I hope you aren't particularly attached to those shoes, princess."

Turning, Jackson swept the water below them to make sure there was nothing she could hurt herself on. He was happy to provide a quick dunking as a lesson, but he didn't want her to get injured.

He knew the moment she realized just what he intended because suddenly she grew about three extra arms.

She began squealing, begging, yelling. Her claws dug into his chest again. He managed to pry off one and then the other, holding both wrists tight in a single hand.

"Stop struggling and take your punishment like a good little thief."

"Jackson, seriously," she panted. "This is barbaric."

"Nothing wrong with a little hazing, princess. We'll call this immersion therapy so maybe the next time you'll think twice about breaking and entering."

Holding her out from his body, Jackson let her hover above the water. Her gaze darted beneath her. She sucked in a hard breath. And then she looked at him with imploring eyes.

"I can't swim."

Something in her gaze almost made him believe her. Or maybe that was just his dick trying to influence him— Mr. Happy wanted her pressed against his body again.

Either way… "Lies aren't going to save you this time, princess."

GOD, SHE WAS going to drown. She'd always known it. Somewhere in the back of her brain, she'd *known* this was her destiny.

Just like it had been her mother's.

Although, unlike her, her mom had loved the water. Had resented giving up her transient life on a ship to take care of a daughter she'd never really wanted.

What irony that on one of the few chances she'd had to go back to it, the water had killed her.

And now it was going to take Loralei.

She stared into Jackson's eyes. They reminded her of the sky at home, bright and blue after a strong summer storm.

But it was clear he didn't believe her. Thought she was lying to save herself a dunking. Well, it wouldn't take him long to realize she was telling the truth. Unfortunately, it would probably be too late.

Jackson swung her body, counted to three as if they were at some frat pool party, and let her go. Air rushed up beside her, the roar filling her ears.

She sucked in a huge breath. The action was automatic. Her eyes clamped closed. It pissed her off that the image tattooed on the back of her lids was of Jackson as he'd sat next to her at the table earlier, looking at her with lust in his eyes and a wicked grin curling his lips.

She was now regretting not letting him take her upstairs and follow through on the promise there.

What kind of screwed up, mixed emotions was she harboring for her murderer?

Her body hit the water ass first, her arms and legs folding up with the pressure of impact. Part of her expected the water to be cold, but it wasn't. It was pleasantly warm, almost soothing.

Her limbs flailed as she sank. Her lungs heaved, bubbles escaping through her nose to drift upward with her descent.

She watched the hull of the ship slip past, just out of reach. Darkness and water closed around her, narrowing her world to the few feet right in front of her.

How long had she been under? It didn't matter.

Her butt hit something solid. Sand clouded up around her, obstructing her vision even more.

Her body lurched. Her lungs burned with the demand to breathe, but somehow she managed to quell the instinct that would have allowed water to fill her lungs.

Dark spots dotted her vision, followed by bright bursts of color.

Something swam in front of her. It would be her luck if it was a shark looking for a quick dinner. Would it be worse to die from drowning or being ripped apart by sharp teeth?

A face appeared in front of her. Jackson. His soft blond hair floated up in a riot, like a lion's mane. His gaze bored into her. He was trying to tell her something, but she didn't have the mental capacity to worry about what it was. A heavy peace settled over her. For the first time she realized just how quiet it was beneath the water. Nothing else mattered.

Was this what her mom had felt right before the end?

She hoped so. So much better than the nightmares she'd been plagued with for years, images of her mom desperate, fighting and in pain.

Something hard wrapped around her chest and she started moving. The darkness began to fade. In some dim corner of her mind, Loralei realized Jackson was towing her to the surface.

Unfortunately, she was afraid it was too late.

Unable to resist the compulsion to breathe any longer, she opened her mouth, searching for air and finding nothing but water.

HOLY HELL, she hadn't been lying.

What on God's green earth was she doing heading up a dive team if she couldn't swim?

Jackson was used to compartmentalizing responses in order to tackle the priorities in front of him. Getting her out of the water was his first point of action. Making sure she was still breathing his second. After that he could decide whether or not to verbally take a strip from her hide.

Later, someone else could take the pound of flesh from his ass for what he'd done.

It had taken him about thirty seconds to realize she wasn't coming up. A few more to convince himself she wasn't playing him for a fool. Another thirty to rocket down to her, snatch her around the waist and start hauling her up to the surface.

Plenty of time. She would be fine.

Because he couldn't live with himself if she actually drowned.

The minx was a thorn in his side, but she didn't deserve to die for that.

Breaking the surface, Jackson shoved her up onto the dock. It was not a good sign that her limbs flopped around uselessly. If she'd passed out, water was definitely in her lungs.

Hauling himself up after her, Jackson rolled her head sideways to clear the water from her mouth and nose. Then he sealed his lips to hers and started mouth-to-mouth. Within a few breaths her chest heaved and she started coughing, water sputtering out. Jackson rolled her, pounded on her back to help get out whatever was left in her lungs.

Her body convulsed with the force of her need to expel the seawater. After several moments, she quieted. Her forehead rested on the rough surface of the dock. Her hand spread out beside her head, hair tangled through her fingers. Her legs were twisted together, as if she didn't have the energy to move a single muscle.

Jackson stopped pounding on her back, instead rubbing up and down in a slow, soothing gesture. He wanted to offer her comfort. But he also kept touching her to reassure himself that she was really breathing.

Finally, Loralei glanced over her shoulder at him. He expected her to yell. He deserved it. Wanted it, so he could find an outlet for the guilt filling his own chest.

What he wasn't prepared for was her sea-roughened voice whispering, "Thank you."

Shit.

"I nearly killed you and you're thanking me?"

"You saved me."

"I threw you in."

Her lips twisted in a half grimace, half smile. "Okay, screw you, asshole. And thanks for saving my life. Feel better now?"

Not particularly. But for some reason he couldn't tell her that. Instead, he lifted her into his arms, heedless of the water that streamed off both of them.

Striding down the dock, he carried her back onto his ship. She stirred, murmured what he knew was going to be the start of a protest, but he cut her off before it could begin.

"Don't bother. You need a shower to warm up. There's

still a chance you could go into shock. And I'm not letting you out of my sight until I know you're not going to develop complications from having your lungs full of water."

He probably should take her to the hospital, but for some reason what he'd said was the truth. He didn't want to let her out of his sight long enough to let anyone else tend to her.

He felt responsible; that was all.

He'd had plenty of experience with water and a few close calls with drowning. If he hadn't felt equipped to recognize a potential problem soon enough to call in reinforcements, he wouldn't be walking her onto his ship.

Apparently, she recognized his resolve because her mouth snapped shut without uttering a single sound.

Carrying her to his stateroom, Jackson moved straight for the tiny attached bathroom. Several of the guys shared one, but as owner, he rated the best room complete with a private bath. Not that it was much. Just a toilet, sink and shower barely big enough to fit his shoulders through.

Shifting her, Jackson let her body slide down his until her feet touched the floor. Water pooled beneath them, but he ignored it.

With one arm still around her waist to steady her, Jackson reached inside the shower and flipped on the faucet to let the water warm.

Drawing back, he stared into her upturned face. Her pale green eyes were a little wary, a little grateful and a lot scared.

Why hadn't he seen that before?

Because he hadn't wanted to believe her.

After pushing back the tangle of black hair from her face, Jackson found himself saying, "I'm sorry," in a gruff voice he barely recognized.

"So am I. I shouldn't have been here. I know you probably won't believe me, but I didn't intend to sneak aboard. Really."

Guilt and uncertainty mixed together in his blood. He wanted to believe her. But he didn't. He couldn't. Not even after almost drowning her.

She'd been telling the truth about not being able to swim, but that didn't mean she wouldn't lie about anything else.

Why did the thought of her doing that hurt?

It shouldn't matter.

This woman was nothing to him. Nothing more than a business rival and the daughter of a man who'd done everything he could to hurt Jackson and his business.

The only thing he could do was shake his head. "It doesn't matter. At least not right now."

Loralei dropped her gaze to the floor between their feet. Her shoulders rose and fell on a deep sigh that he felt more than heard.

She took a half step backward—about as much room as she could force between them—and dropped her hands from their resting place against his chest.

Steam began to fill the tiny room, billowing out around the glass shower enclosure. It turned the air around them muggy and heavy.

Without raising her gaze, Loralei reached for the buttons on her shirt. Until that moment he hadn't noticed just how thin and clingy it was. Earlier, it had looked big and breezy, swirling around her body and hiding the curves he'd instinctively known were beneath it.

Now, those curves were seriously on display. The gauzy material was plastered to her body and practically see-through.

"Go away, Jackson, so I can take my shower, get off this boat and back to my hotel."

She popped a single button, but he didn't move.

"Ship. She's a ship."

Another one went. "Whatever."

It wasn't as if she was revealing anything he couldn't already almost see. But Jackson couldn't tear away his gaze as she slowly, meticulously revealed each inch of golden skin. He stayed where he was until she reached her breasts, which swelled round and inviting over the edge of white lace.

Spinning on his heel, Jackson bolted for the bedroom, his own lungs heaving as if he'd been the one to cough up a gallon of seawater.

He raked his fingers through his hair, shook off the water that still clung to him, not caring what got wet in the process. Behind him, the bathroom door closed with a quiet click.

The barrier didn't help. He could hear her moving around in the small space. Imagine her standing in his shower, using his shampoo and running her soap-covered hands over her naked body.

After yanking off his own wet clothes, he donned dry ones and pulled out an old T-shirt and gym shorts for her.

He wanted to escape above deck before he did something stupid. Such as tear the bathroom door off its hinges so he could help her rinse away the suds. He even started to leave, but he couldn't make himself go. Not until he knew she was actually okay.

So instead he began to prowl the small space, an uncomfortable sensation tingling at the back of his neck. The longer Loralei stayed in that room, the worse it became. He started worrying, remembering how she'd looked lying on the dock, eerily still and lifeless.

Break in the door or wait?

He'd never been one for indecision, but tonight he couldn't make up his mind.

Which only frustrated him more.

4

LORALEI WRAPPED HER arms around her body and held on tight. Despite the warm water rushing over her, she shivered.

Closing her eyes, she let her head drop against the fiberglass wall in front of her. Then she just stood there with a jumble of thoughts and pictures running in an endless loop through her brain. She'd almost died. Drowned. The helpless sensation she'd felt as she'd looked up through the water and realized she couldn't do anything to save herself… It had sucked.

What was wrong with her? She was an adult. She shouldn't be ruled by her fear like a child afraid of the dark.

It sucked even worse that Jackson Duchane had been the one to rescue her.

God, her lips still tingled where he'd pressed his mouth to hers and breathed life back into her lungs. Every nerve ending in her body was alive from the sensation of being carried by him. That chest. Those shoulders. She'd gotten a front-and-center introduction to the hard body hidden beneath his clothes.

And she wanted more.

Seriously, what was wrong with her?

Realizing the trembling had finally stopped, Loralei quickly picked up the single bottle sitting on the shelf and dumped a huge dollop of shampoo into her hand. A clean, crisp scent melted into the small space around her. Without thinking, she pulled in a deep breath. She already associated the salt and sandalwood combination with the man who'd saved her life.

Part of her wanted to curl into a ball in the corner of his shower, give in to the black pit of fear that was threatening at the edges of her consciousness. But she refused to succumb to the temptation.

Rinsing the residue of saltwater from her skin, she finally stepped from the comfort of the steam-filled space. She grabbed a towel and swiped it across her dripping hair several times before wrapping it around her body.

Glancing around, she realized she had nothing to put on.

Great.

It wasn't bad enough that she had to face him, now she was going to have to do it wearing nothing but a scrap of terrycloth that barely covered her from chest to hip.

After sucking in a deep, calming breath, Loralei straightened her shoulders and reached for the door handle.

One step into the attached bedroom her bravado failed her and she froze.

Jackson was stalking around the small space. Tension radiated off his tight body. His hands were threaded together at the base of his neck, his back and shoulder muscles rippled against a T-shirt that looked well-worn and soft enough to wrap a newborn baby in.

Jesus. No man should look like that. Loralei's heart slammed into her throat before dropping to her toes. Her stomach rolled, not from fear or the rocking ship, but from a burst of lust that nearly knocked her on her ass.

And that was before he turned around and raked her with those summer-blue eyes. Oh, shit. The intensity in his gaze had her swaying on her feet. Her body tingled, jumped to life. Beneath the thin layer of cotton, her nipples tightened into aching points, reminding her just how naked and vulnerable she was.

Before she could attempt to get a grip on her runaway libido, he was standing beside her. How had he moved so quickly?

The heat of his huge hand settled on her arm, steadying her.

"Easy," he murmured. His voice, deep and rough, scraped across her senses.

"I was about to bust in there. You were taking a long time."

Loralei stared up at him, surprised to see genuine concern swirling together with guilt. And lust. Dammit, that wasn't helping her runaway hormones. Especially when the vision of him slipping into that tiny shower with her ghosted across her thoughts.

Shaking away temptation, Loralei licked her lips and said, "I'm fine."

Was that really her voice? All scratchy and fragile?

His gorgeous mouth pulled down at the edges in a frown. Why did she suddenly have the urge to reach out and run the pad of her finger across his lips? Would they be as hard as the rest of him, or soft and yielding?

"Why don't I believe you?"

"Seriously." She had to get a grip...on something other than him. Stepping away, Loralei watched his hand drop to his side. Already, she missed the comforting warmth that had spread through her from where he'd touched. "Hand me some clothes so I can head back to my hotel room."

Jackson twisted and grabbed a pile from the small table beside the bed. Instead of holding them out to her, he pressed them against his chest and folded his arms over them. The veins running along his biceps pulsed.

"You're not going anywhere."

His words were the catalyst she needed to drag her gaze back to his stony expression.

"Of course I am. I need to get back to my crew."

"What you need to do is rest."

"Exactly. And the sooner you give me those the sooner I can get out of your hair." Loralei held out her hand hoping he'd plop the clothes against her palm. He didn't, but she kept her arm out anyway.

His expression turned harsh, those amazing eyes going as sharp as cut glass. She could see the argument coming and felt her own body respond, adrenaline surging into her already spinning system.

But before she could say anything, his entire body changed. All the tension bled out of him. His mouth softened. Tiny lines crinkled the edges of his eyes, which had melted into pools of heat.

Tossing the clothes back onto the bed behind him, he took a single step forward and filled her personal space. But he didn't touch her. Was it wrong that she wished he had?

Instead, he laced his fingers behind his neck again.

"Loralei, you nearly drowned."

Just those few simple words had the ghost of her panic welling inside her again.

"I know," she whispered.

"I have to keep an eye on you. Make sure you don't have

any complications. There are plenty of reports of people dying hours after a near drowning."

Loralei swallowed. That wasn't exactly what she wanted to hear right now, but she'd deal with that unpleasant thought later. Right now she had to convince this man to step back and let her go.

Or she wasn't sure she'd be able to keep herself from reaching out and running her hands over his wide chest and shoulders.

"My crew can keep an eye on me. Tell me what to look for."

She barely got out the words before he was shaking his head. "I threw you in. Even after you told me you couldn't swim. You're my responsibility."

One thing made her hesitate. If she went back to her room she'd have to explain to Brian what had happened and why he had to keep an eye on her to make sure she was okay. He'd find out her secret.

It was bad enough Jackson knew she couldn't swim. She really didn't need any of her crew finding out. She was already the outsider, with little knowledge about how a diving ship operated.

Loralei pulled her lower lip into her mouth and worried it with her teeth as indecision twisted through her gut. She hated not knowing what to do.

Using his thumb, Jackson eased her lip away from the self-inflicted torture.

"You're safe here, Loralei. I promise you."

Maybe she was safe from him. Her mouth was tingling where he'd touched her. Waves of sensation radiated from the single, innocuous spot.

But who was going to protect her from herself?

HE REALLY HAD to get some clothes on the woman. He'd never noticed that his towel was particularly small, but the knot she'd twisted it into between her breasts was unraveling centimeter by centimeter, giving him a bigger glimpse of her smooth, tanned skin.

Her black hair curled damply around her shoulders in a riot of tangles that made him want to bury his hands in it and use it to pull her face closer so he could taste her lips again.

What the hell?

He seriously needed to get a grip.

Turning away, he snatched up the shorts and shirt he'd tossed onto the bed for her. He whipped back around and collided with her.

Her hands landed on his chest. Her body crashed against him. Pressed tight between them, he felt the towel's knot finally give way. Just as his control was doing. In a desperate attempt to save them both, Jackson grabbed for the towel as it slid down her back. The instinctive move backfired. Big time.

His fingers brushed across her naked skin. She gasped and arched into him. The soft curve of her breasts flattened against the hard plane of his body even as the towel was caught between them.

God, he wanted more.

They both stilled, locked in the precarious position and certain one wrong move could bring disaster crashing down on them both.

Unfortunately, Jackson wasn't sure which would be the disaster: letting her go or not letting her go. The waters definitely had been muddied.

Slowly, Loralei tipped her head back and dragged her gaze up to meet his.

Damn, her eyes were deep. Deep enough he could dive inside and get lost. And the way she was staring at him made his stomach knot and his cock throb.

She licked her lips, parted them as if she was going to say something, but nothing came out. She inhaled deeply, her chest rising and falling against the edge of the towel that flirted with the sharp peaks of her nipples.

Jackson had to close his eyes at the sensation of her body moving against his. He was only human.

"Loralei," he murmured, keeping his eyes shut tight. "Step back. Now."

If he was strong enough, he'd be the one to turn away. But he had only a slippery hold on his control right now, and if he moved Jackson was seriously afraid it would be in the wrong direction. This was his last-ditch effort at doing the right thing, because in about five seconds he wasn't going to be able to curb his response to her anymore.

But she didn't move.

"Seriously," he growled.

Every muscle in his body was tight with the effort to hold himself in check. He felt…brittle. On the edge of exploding.

And he wasn't particularly enamored with the sensation.

Jackson prided himself on his self-control. He'd fought hard for the ability to withstand the harshest conditions without cracking.

But sixty seconds with this woman pressed tight against him and every hard-won victory had disappeared like so much smoke.

"What if I don't want to move?" she finally whispered.

Jackson groaned. His eyes popped open as his fingers, which were pressed against her back, flexed in preparation for digging in and taking more.

He stared at her, searching her expression for some sign that she meant what she'd just said.

Rising onto the tips of her toes, she wrapped her hands

around his neck and urged him toward her. Just before her lips touched his she whispered, "Remind me that I'm alive."

The minute their mouths collided it was over. He'd have to worry about the aftermath later, because he was too preoccupied to give a damn about anything but the taste and feel of her.

His hands slipped into her hair, angled her head so he could have better access to her hot mouth.

The moment was complete combustion. Their tongues tangled. She bounced on her toes, as if trying to get more of him. Without breaking their connection, Jackson wrapped an arm around her waist and hauled her higher.

They both forgot about the towel. It snagged, hanging between them unnoticed. Jackson ran his palms across the slope of her back. Her skin was still damp from her shower. So smooth and soft. He could spend hours just touching her.

Even as his mouth devoured hers, his hands studied and learned. The way her body arched into his touch when he skimmed the sensitive dip right above her rear. Or the tiny catch in her breath that he drank in as he caressed between her shoulder blades.

He wanted to take a step back and appreciate the view, but she wouldn't let him. Her hands were everywhere. Her rush to consume him only managed to fuel his own raging need.

Loralei broke the kiss, but only long enough to run her mouth over the skin of his neck, taking teasing licks before sucking gently. The tug of her lips arrowed straight down to where his cock leaped against the fly of the jeans he'd thrown on.

Why had he bothered? He couldn't remember anymore. Twisting, he pressed her up against the first available surface, which just happened to be the edge of the dresser. Reaching blindly behind her, Loralei managed to swipe her hand over the top, clearing the few random things that were scattered there. They pinged against the floor, but he didn't care. They weren't important anyway.

Jackson pulled back, relishing her broken little pants as she tried to catch her breath. The towel was draped across her body, tucked between her legs. In the mirror behind her, he could see the hard swell of her ass. Her skin glowed.

She watched him out of eyes glazed with desire. He wanted that, liked knowing he could make her feel that way. "Jackson, please."

But her fractured words also had a spike of ice arrowing straight through him. What had she said?

Remind me I'm alive.

He wanted to do just that. Remind them both. But he shouldn't. Taking a step away from her, Jackson tried to regain his sanity. Make his brain re-engage.

"What are you doing?"

He shook his head, hating the way her eyes slowly refocused on the here and now instead of the pleasure he'd been giving her moments ago.

"You…" Jackson balled his hands into fists. "This isn't what you need right now."

Loralei's mouth pulled into a tight line. "Don't you dare."

"Don't I dare what?"

Reaching out, Loralei balled her fists into his T-shirt, using the leverage to haul him closer.

"Walk away from me again tonight."

Every pulse point in his body throbbed. Jackson stared down at her upturned face, trying desperately not to notice her half-naked body before him.

Gently, he reached up and unwrapped her fingers, one by one, from his shirt.

Placing her hand on the dresser beside her hip, he wrapped her fingers over the edge, holding her hand in place...and away from him.

"Goddamn you," she breathed.

Her eyes sparked and beneath that smooth caramel color her skin flushed red.

Before he could react, her other hand flashed out, cupping his obvious reaction to what they'd just been doing.

"You want this as much as I do."

Of course he wanted her. She was beautiful. Just as he was certain the apple offered by the serpent in the Garden of Eden had been beautiful. "Yeah, I want you."

"Then why are you backing away?"

"Because it's the right thing to do."

She laughed, the brittle sound ripping through his chest.

Planting her hands on him, Loralei pushed. Jackson took several steps backward, for her and himself. She hopped down and he tried damn hard not to notice the way her lithe muscles rippled with the movement.

Using her arms to hold the towel tight against her, Loralei reached for the edge and wrapped it back around her body, studiously ignoring him the entire time. She stalked over to the bed and snatched up the clothes before she disappeared into the bathroom and slammed the door.

Jackson waited, hands clasped behind his neck. It wasn't long before she barreled back out. Her hair hung like wet ropes down her back. Damp patches were already spreading across the shoulders of his T-shirt, which was so big on her the neck hung off one shoulder and the hem flared around her thighs. He knew she was wearing a pair of his shorts underneath, but he couldn't see them.

Something about seeing her all rumpled and angry in

his clothes made his chest tighten and his blood pump just a bit faster.

Without a word, she turned for the door. It wasn't necessary to tell him what she intended. It was written all over her face. Luckily, he was faster. His palm slammed against the flat panel of the door before she managed to get it open an inch.

"Where do you think you're going?"

"Back to my hotel," she bit out through clenched teeth, still refusing to look at him.

"I already told you that wasn't happening, princess."

"So, what? You're going to keep me prisoner? Pretty sure that's called kidnapping, ace."

Crowding into her personal space, Jackson loomed over her. He didn't touch her. He didn't have to. She instinctively moved away from him, pressing her body into the door.

"A few minutes ago you were begging to stay."

She shrugged. "Not anymore."

5

JACKSON LEANED A shoulder against the door and crossed his arms loosely over his chest. "You've got two choices, princess. One, you stay here where I can keep an eye on you."

Her mouth thinned and her eyes flashed. Was it wrong that he liked it when she was angry?

"Or...?"

"Or I take you to the nearest hospital where they keep you under observation."

"Option two."

Shrugging, Jackson said, "Suit yourself."

Reaching behind him, he picked up his wallet, which had been swept to the floor in their earlier frenzy. Stuffing it into his pocket, he kicked around a few things until he found the keys to the rental parked in the marina lot.

Putting his hand on her back, Jackson tried to lead her out of the room, but she jerked away from him.

"Don't."

A few minutes ago she hadn't been able to get enough of his hands on her body, but he didn't think now was the time to point that out. Not unless he wanted to be occupying the bed next to her in the ER nursing a broken nose.

As she stalked down the hall in front of him, he found

it difficult not to notice the sway of her hips or the way his clothes hung on her lithe body.

She probably wouldn't appreciate him commenting on that, either. Now if Asher had been with them, he would have been spouting inappropriate remarks left and right. And getting away with it by doing it in a way that had everyone around them—Loralei included—laughing. The man had a talent for putting people at ease that Jackson had always envied.

They reached the deck. Her stride faltered. Her body just…froze. Thinking back on the events of the night, Jackson realized that must have been what had happened when he'd found her crouched and clinging to the railing, her gaze trained on the water.

She wasn't just afraid of the water. She was terrified.

Scooping her into his arms, Jackson tucked her against his body.

"You still choose option two?"

Nodding, Loralei whispered, "Get me off this ship. Please."

The tremble in her voice was real. Something about it kicked his protective instincts into overdrive.

Women and children in need—they always got to him. It wasn't that he thought Loralei was incapable of taking care of herself. The sticky drink residue he'd had to wash off earlier was proof she could hold her own.

But right now she looked a hell of a lot more vulnerable than made him comfortable.

It didn't take them long to reach the ER. The moment he'd settled her into the passenger seat of the Jeep he'd rented, her body had begun to relax. Maybe it was because they weren't on the water any longer.

Still, he'd been relieved when she'd dropped her head back against the seat and closed her eyes. Her chest had risen and fallen with steady breaths. For a few minutes he'd wondered if maybe she'd fallen asleep, but that question was answered when they pulled into the parking lot.

He no sooner parked than she was bolting from the car...and walking in the opposite direction of the front door.

Bounding out, Jackson snagged her arm and swung her back the other way. "Where do you think you're going?"

"Back to my hotel."

"Oh, no you don't. You agreed to be checked out."

She glared up at him, her green eyes flashing with a fire that rekindled the heat in his blood. "I changed my mind. This is stupid, Jackson. I'm fine."

"Here's the thing, princess," he drawled. "I'm not opposed to making a scene in this parking lot."

She crossed her arms over her chest, her gaze fairly taunting him, and said, "Go ahead."

The blood at the base of his skull began to throb with irritation and a thin thread of excitement he didn't really want to admit feeling.

Slowly, he let a dangerous grin touch his lips. "If that's the way you want to do this..."

Grasping her behind the knees and shoulders, Jackson cradled her against his body and sprinted for the doors of the ER. They swished open with a muted hiss. Before they were half open, he was already hollering at the top of his lungs.

"Someone help me! My wife nearly drowned."

Loralei struggled in his arms, but he simply tightened his hold, careful not to actually hurt her. That wasn't easy considering she was putting everything she had into getting free.

"Jackson, stop it," she hissed.

Leaning close, he whispered in her ear, "I offered you the easy way, princess."

Several people dressed in scrubs—nurses he guessed—came running.

"What's wrong?" the one in the lead asked.

"He's overreacting," Loralei tried to say, but her voice got lost in the din.

"My wife fell off our ship in the harbor. She might have hit her head."

Loralei gasped. "I didn't hit my head and you know it."

Someone rolled up a gurney. Jackson transferred her onto it, making sure to keep a hand on her even as a couple nurses crowded around her.

"She was unconscious when I reached her. I pulled her out and did mouth-to-mouth." He ran his hand down her still damp hair, tangling his fingers in the strands in a possessive and familiar gesture. "She coughed up a lot of water," he said, letting his eyes fill with concern.

It wasn't completely a lie. He had been concerned. Was still worried about the potential for complications.

"I'm fine," Loralei protested, trying to push herself up and off the gurney.

"Please lie still, Mrs…"

"Miss. Lancaster. And this man isn't my husband."

Jackson let his eyebrows beetle, shaking his head as he turned to one of the nurses. "Could the disorientation be from hitting her head?"

As they wheeled her away, Jackson could hear Loralei's squeal of frustration.

A nurse took his arm and led him behind them. "We'll take good care of your wife, sir. I have a few forms for you to complete…"

LORALEI WAS GOING to kill him.

"Your husband is adorable," one of the nurses said,

fussing around her as they placed a cuff on her arm and a little doohickey on her finger.

"He isn't my husband."

"Too bad. He's scrumptious."

She could think of a few choice words to describe Jackson Duchane right now and scrumptious wasn't anywhere close to the top one hundred. But before she could snap back a comment, a doctor bustled into the tiny room. He had gorgeous dark skin and a no-nonsense attitude as he scanned her chart and began an exam.

After listening to her lungs, he turned to the nurse and said, "Let's get a chest X-ray and run a CBC." Turning to her, he said, "I'm going to want to keep you overnight for observation."

That's when Loralei started pulling at all the lines connecting her to the machines in the room.

"No."

"No?" the doctor said, his expression saying he didn't understand the simple word.

"No. No X-rays, blood work or staying overnight. I feel absolutely fine. My…friend is being paranoid."

"No, he isn't, ma'am. There's a very real possibility for you to experience complications."

Everyone in the room was staring at her as if she'd gone completely crazy. Maybe she really had. This had turned into the day from hell and she didn't think she could handle one more minute of sitting in this hospital bed wearing the paper-thin gown they'd given her.

"I promise I'm fine," she said for what felt like the thousandth time. Why would no one listen to her?

"I was only under for a few seconds. I'm breathing okay, no pain or pressure." Loralei just wanted this nightmare to end. It was bad enough that Jackson had witnessed her panic and paralyzing fear.

Couldn't everyone just forget the whole damn thing had happened?

The doctor's mouth thinned. "If you're insistent on leaving you'll have to sign a form that you're doing it against medical advice."

"Fine." She'd sign whatever they wanted. It was damn late. Probably closing in on two in the morning and she was exhausted.

Shaking his head, the doctor spun on his heel, charging straight for the next emergency that waited for him. The rest of the staff cleared out leaving her blessedly alone for what felt like the first time in hours.

After sliding from the bed, Loralei leaned over to pick up the clothes someone had folded and put on the chair in the corner. A low, appreciative whistle sounded behind her.

Straightening, she spun, tugging at the gown to make it cover more of her body than it was.

Jackson filled the doorway. Arms crossed over his chest, one of his shoulders propped against the jamb, he frowned at her.

The expression sent an unwelcome shiver through her—awareness tinged with a bit of apprehension. It was hard to miss the soldier lurking beneath the relaxed facade. He could keep her inside this room and probably do it without breaking a sweat.

"They said you're refusing medical treatment."

Loralei yanked her shorts on beneath the gown. "Yes."

"Why would you do a stupid thing like that?"

Bent at the waist, she glared up at him. "Because I'm not sick," she ground out. "I don't want X-rays or blood tests. And I sure as hell can't afford a night in a hospital that most definitely isn't in my network."

"I filled out your paperwork and agreed to cover your expenses."

What the hell. "Why would you do that?"

"Because I'm the reason you're in here."

God, she didn't want to appreciate the gesture or the fact that he was taking responsibility for what he'd done. But she did.

Which made it twice as hard to forget the wanton way she'd thrown herself at him not an hour ago. And the way he'd politely said no.

"Look, it's been a hell of a long day. I had to get up at the butt-crack of dawn to make my flight this morning. I've been awake for almost twenty hours at this point. All I want right now is a soft bed and about a day of uninterrupted sleep."

Unfortunately, she'd be lucky to get in a solid four hours before she had to be up and back on the *Emily*.

Her muscles seized at just the thought of being back on that ship, surrounded by water.

Closing her eyes, Loralei tried to will away the panic attack she could feel lurking at the edges of her consciousness.

"How about a compromise?" His gentle voice, closer than she expected, startled her.

Loralei's eyes popped open to find Jackson standing before her. His hands hung loosely by his sides, but he watched her with that sharp gaze that saw way too much.

"Let them take the X-rays and run the blood work. If everything looks fine, then I'll take you back to your hotel. An hour at the most." He paused, rocked back on his heels and shoved his hands deep into the pockets of his worn jeans. "Please."

Something about the way he said the word made her think he didn't use it often. He struck her more as the kind of man used to issuing orders and having them followed.

The doctor's words tumbled through her head.

"I'm not staying the night."

"Okay, you don't have to stay."

"And I'm not wearing the damn gown."

Jackson chuckled, the sound tickling across her senses. "Fair enough."

He leaned his head out the door and spoke softly to someone who'd obviously been waiting on the other side.

She sagged against the edge of the bed. Suddenly, she was certain she was going to regret giving in to him.

JACKSON WAS RELIEVED Loralei didn't appear to have any lasting effects from her near drowning.

The doctor had said her chest film was clear, her oxygen levels fine.

It had taken slightly more than the hour he'd promised, which Loralei would get over.

He had no idea how she was still awake. And not just awake, but wired. It could have had something to do with the diet soda she'd been mainlining since the doctor had told her she could have something to drink.

Maybe Jackson should have listened to her and let her leave when she'd wanted. Then they both would be in their own beds, asleep and decidedly less annoyed.

But for some reason he couldn't make himself leave.

His crew was expecting to ship out bright and early in the morning, which would be in a couple hours. Not that he couldn't handle a single night without sleep. He'd experienced worse conditions in some of the grittiest shit holes in the world. In comparison, this was a walk in the park.

After pulling into the circular drive of her hotel, Jackson stopped right outside the entrance. She didn't wait for him to come around, but got out and slammed the door shut behind her before stalking away.

Jackson planted his rear against the side of the car and watched her through the huge wall of glass that now separated them. Half way across the lobby, she came to a halt, seeming to stare at the bank of elevators on the far side. He watched her shoulders rise and fall on a deep breath. Then she dropped her head back and looked up at the ceiling. What the heck was she doing?

A moment later he found himself inside the lobby, standing beside her and trying to make out the words she was muttering under her breath.

"What's wrong?" he asked.

"I lost my room key." She turned. He expected to be treated to another of her patented glares, but instead was met with pure exhaustion shining out of puffy eyes. She was running on fumes and probably had been for the past hour, caffeine and soda masking the truth. "When I nearly drowned."

Aw, hell.

"And my ID is upstairs."

Without saying another word, he walked over to the front desk and, with an apologetic smile, started explaining the situation to the nice woman working reception at three in the morning.

Luckily, the woman had been on duty when Loralei checked in late in the afternoon so remembered her and was willing to reissue her key.

Grasping her hand, Jackson slapped the piece of plastic against her palm, curled her fingers over it and took a step toward the door.

Escape. That's what he wanted.

So he couldn't explain why he didn't actually walk out the door until the elevator Loralei disappeared into closed between them.

6

LORALEI WAS FRUSTRATED…with herself and her team. She was exhausted, cranky and on edge. She was trying desperately to hold it together so that she wouldn't hyperventilate every time her gaze swept across the deck and the vast blue ocean surrounding them.

A battle she was seriously afraid she was going to lose eventually.

And then what?

The last thing she needed was for her team to figure out she couldn't handle being this close to the water. They were already reluctant to listen to anything she had to say, treating her like a little kid instead of their boss.

"No, Brian, I am not going to argue with you about this again. I want to go here." Loralei stabbed a short nail at the map showing an inlet on the far side of a tiny island.

"But…" Brian sputtered.

They'd been having this argument for the past fifteen minutes.

"No buts, Brian. Is this my ship?"

He frowned, his eyebrows snapping together as his light brown eyes flashed. Loralei was too pissed herself to heed the warning.

"Yes."

"Great. I've done the research."

And she had. The minute she'd uncovered the information on the *Chimera*, stuffed into the back of a filing cabinet in her father's office, she'd been intrigued.

It was the kind of story that grabbed her attention. Add in the Civil War angle…cat nip for any professor of American history. The American Revolution was her specialty, but that didn't stop her from appreciating the impact the Civil War had had on the country.

And how easily the outcome could have changed at any point in the struggle.

She'd quickly gotten lost in the material she'd discovered, wanting to learn more. It hadn't taken her long to slip down the rabbit hole of research.

The *Chimera* had a varied history. Initially she had been a cargo ship, running trade routes between Europe, China and the West Indies. Somewhere along the way a major plantation owner in the French West Indies had purchased the ship and settled into transporting goods and people between the islands and America.

She had been profitable, right up until the Civil War had interfered with the market for luxury goods. However, the plantation owner, with family and land in Georgia himself, had had a stake in the outcome of the war. And influence over many powerful, rich friends in the Caribbean. He'd rallied support from the other merchants and plantation owners, who had feared a change in the slave culture in America could negatively impact their own way of life on the islands.

Supplies and munitions had been gathered. Money had been quietly raised. And everything had been loaded onto the *Chimera*, a ship that routinely ran the route and had the experience and crew to slip past the blockades.

Unfortunately, she never made it that far.

According to an eyewitness report from a boy from the surrounding islands, the *Chimera* had anchored in the inlet hours before the hurricane that sunk her had hit. Most historians discounted the statement. In order for the *Chimera* to have been there, she would have been days off course even before the threat of the storm.

Loralei wasn't in the habit of discounting anything, especially considering the *Chimera* had been lost for such a long time.

"Take us there, Brian. Now," Loralei ordered, slamming her palm down over the map and glaring up at him.

Teeth grinding together, Brian spun on his heel and headed out of the little room she'd commandeered to spread out her research materials.

She wasn't convinced this was the place where the *Chimera* had sunk. In fact, she'd be more surprised if they found her than if they didn't. But it was a starting point. There were still several leads she wanted to run down.

Just the thought of getting lost inside the old documents and historical records gave her a tiny, giddy thrill.

Confident Brian would follow her instructions, at least for now, Loralei popped the lid of her laptop and called up a site she often used for research.

One plus to staying glued to her computer was that for those few hours, tucked in a room below deck, she could almost forget she was on a ship.

At least until the *Emily* pitched, and Loralei was thrown off balance for a few seconds before the ship righted herself.

Her stomach rolled. Loralei squeezed her eyes shut.

And the first thing she saw was Jackson's calm, steady gaze as he'd watched her last night on the dock, water dripping from his hair and face, concern and guilt clouding his eyes.

Nope, not what she needed right now.

"WE HAVE COMPANY."

Marcus's shout from the helm had frustration pouring into Jackson's blood stream.

Biting back the foul language desperate to escape, he tossed down the equipment he'd been inspecting in preparation for taking the team out, crossed the deck and climbed the ladder to the helm.

"What the hell are you talking about?"

"Pretty sure that's Lancaster's ship," Marcus said, pointing out the glassed-in window to starboard.

He growled beneath his breath. "What the hell is she doing here?"

This inlet hadn't been on any of the documents James Lancaster had stolen from him.

Had she gotten a look at his newest information before he'd found her crouched on the deck? Not possible. Or at least he'd convinced himself of that.

Since Lancaster had broken in he'd been more careful with his research. And Loralei Lancaster hadn't struck him as the kind of woman with B-and-E skills in her back pocket.

Swearing again under his breath, Jackson fought back the urge to hit something. Apparently he'd been wrong.

Why the hell had he given her the benefit of the doubt? Believed her when she'd looked up at him with those wide green eyes and said she was sorry.

He'd let his libido convince him. Hell, she'd probably used that against him, too. Thinking back, she was the one who'd initiated that steamy kiss in his room, all wet and tempting and practically naked.

She'd known exactly what she was doing.

Letting any part of him hope she wasn't like her father was just stupid. It was a lesson he wouldn't forget again.

Jackson stared out across the bright blue water. Crap. There wasn't a thing he could do about it now that Loralei's team was here. Luckily, he didn't think the *Chimera* had actually gone down in the inlet, only that she'd been here before the hurricane hit.

But he believed in covering all the bases. And following the leads as they came. Since the last eyewitness testimony he'd uncovered had the *Chimera* here, that was where they were starting their search.

As much as he wanted to bar her from diving on the site, Jackson didn't have the power to do that. He needed to make sure his team was down first and uncovered anything of value so that he could keep the information to himself.

Spinning for the door, he was back on the deck with his team in record time.

"Hurry up, boys. We have work to do and I'm not a fan of wasting daylight. Get your equipment checked and prepped, and get your asses in the water."

Marcus sent him a knowing grin. Chad offered him a small salute, but used a strategic finger to do it. The rest of the team simply put their heads down and went to work.

He didn't care that he was taking out his foul mood on them. They were tough. They'd survive.

"We've got company and I don't want them getting their hands on something that's ours."

That lit a fire under some butts, because these guys were as invested in finding the *Chimera* as he was. As part of the discovery team, they stood to make a nice, tidy bonus when they uncovered her. They weren't any more enamored than he was with the idea of someone else beating them to the punch.

Out of the corner of his eye, Jackson saw *Emily's Fortune* pull in about forty yards away and anchor.

Positioned on the diving platform on the back of the ship, he paused for several moments, scanning the decks. He wasn't looking for a glimpse of Loralei because he wanted to see her beautiful, treacherous face. No, all he wanted to do was let her know she was in for a fight.

There. As far away from the railing along the deck as she could possibly get, she stood. Her legs were spread wide against the gentle pitch and roll of the deck, her knees soft as she unconsciously compensated for the motion.

But he noticed she didn't once look at the water around her. Her face was pinched, her eyes squinting against the bright glare of sunlight.

Maybe she felt his eyes on her. Or maybe she was looking for him as he'd been looking for her. But he knew the moment their gazes collided. Felt the impact of it straight through to his bones…not to mention in his groin, which tightened painfully inside his wetsuit.

Crossing his arms over his chest, he stared at her as his men splashed into the water behind him. Then, when it was his turn, he offered her a bastardized salute, obviously unwilling to give her the real thing. With that one gesture, he managed to call her a coward, a thief and issue a little friendly provocation.

Right before falling backward into the water.

HEAT DID NOT blast through her when Jackson Duchane stared at her across the space between their ships.

She wouldn't let it.

It was clear the man was angry with her. She could read it in his stiff body language and the half-assed gesture he'd given her before falling into the water. What she couldn't tell was why… He had a few things to choose from. Was he upset about what had happened last night? Was he pissed she'd shown up at his dive site? Or was he angry over something else she hadn't thought of yet?

She didn't have the luxury of time or energy to care. Not when she was hanging on to her control by a thin thread.

Although, that tight smirk he'd tossed her before disappearing beneath the glassy surface of the water had done one thing for her—it had helped steel her spine.

She had to get her shit together so that she could beat his arrogant ass to the *Chimera*. He couldn't win. Her dad would be so disappointed if she let him.

This was the man who'd almost drowned her. He wasn't nice. Her father hadn't liked him. She needed to remember that and not get caught up in his pretty face and amazing body.

Even if he had saved her. And insisted on taking care of her.

But those things didn't negate his other actions.

All around her, the team bustled with activity. They were pulling out equipment, setting up everything for the dive. And she stood in the middle of it feeling useless and helpless. She had no idea what any of them were doing. And up until that moment, she'd thought she had no desire to learn.

But now wasn't the time to slow them down with questions. Not when Jackson's team was already in the water.

She heard the splash as several men with tanks strapped to their backs dropped into the sea. She simply stood there, waiting. Several members of the team were on deck to monitor the equipment. They watched the feed from cameras the divers had taken down to survey the ocean floor and checked in with them regularly.

All she could think about was her mom's accident down there beneath the cool blue water.

Jackson. Brian. The rest of her team. They were all down there, as far as she was concerned taking risks. That realization made her stomach flip uncomfortably.

Knowing there was nothing for her to do up here but wait, Loralei headed below deck to do the one thing she could to contribute—continue her research.

It was hours later when an excited shout dragged her back to the present. Loud feet slapped the deck above her head. Her first instinct was to assume something was wrong. Heart pounding, Loralei rushed out and up, bracing for whatever disaster she was about to face.

Instead of blood or fear, she found several of her team members whooping and hollering with glee, huge smiles on their faces.

She watched a hydraulic arm at the back of the boat swing from the water out over the deck and lower something down. Minutes later the whirring sounded again as the heavy cables rolled back, revealing a solid object covered with barnacles and brine. It was cylindrical, larger on one end than the other.

"It's a cannon," Brian said from beside her. She hadn't even realized he'd walked close.

"Eric needs to clean it up, preserve it, but it should have identifying markings. We're hoping it belonged to the *Chimera*."

Her father had contracted with Eric Tapscott only days before his heart attack. He was a preservation specialist and, looking over his credentials, had seemed like a great addition to the team, so Loralei had kept him on. She was about to find out if he was worth the money she was paying him considering she really couldn't afford it.

Drawn by the object and excitement that ran through

her crew, Loralei took several steps closer. Her gaze trained on the huge piece of ancient weaponry.

"It's the right shape and size for the time period," she said, almost to herself. Walking around it, she crouched down, but couldn't see much of anything through the layers of filth the ocean had deposited.

As a history professor she spent most of her out-of-class time between stacks of dusty books or with her fingers flying over a keyboard. It wasn't often she got this close to artifacts from the past, although whenever she did, the thrill was electrifying.

At one point she'd considered taking her degree and going to work for one of the major history museums. But the call of research and the joy of teaching had been too great to resist.

Still, that didn't stop the surge of excitement that snaked through her body. Even if it wasn't from the *Chimera*, it was a piece of history that her team had just reclaimed from the deep.

A jagged crack ran down the barrel of the cannon. "You figure it was broken before or cracked when it hit bottom?" Brian asked.

Loralei shrugged. There was no way to know for certain but… "Why carry this heavy sucker if it was useless?" From her crouched position she looked up at her team all gathered around. "Did you find any other signs of wreckage down there?"

Slowly, several of the guys shook their heads.

Of course not. It couldn't be that easy. If they'd found the Chimera their first day out Loralei would have dropped to the deck in a faint.

The ship had been lost for a hundred and fifty years. Others had searched for her—soon after her loss and later.

Treasure hunters who'd all obviously been looking in the wrong places.

This gave her hope and soothed the desperation she was trying valiantly to ignore. She felt it in her bones—this was a huge find, something necessary if she wanted to keep Lancaster Diving afloat.

"All right, guys. Let's get this preserved and cleaned up. We need to know for sure if it belonged to the *Chimera*."

The reality was any number of ships could have dropped that cannon into the waters of this inlet.

HOURS LATER, JACKSON was still grinding his teeth at the thought of Loralei's team finding that damn cannon. It chafed. A lot.

He'd spent years studying and searching, only to have the first potential find from the *Chimera* go to someone else.

From yards away he'd watched Loralei's team uncover the cannon half submerged in the sandy ocean floor. Frustration and anger had seared through him. He'd surfaced just in time to hear shouts of victory filling the air—that hadn't helped his mood. And it hadn't improved much since then.

He'd been stalking around the ship in such a snit that Marcus had pointed him in the direction of their launch boats and not so politely told him to take a break before the rest of the team decided to mutiny.

Of course, he'd ignored the suggestion. Part of owning Trident meant he no longer had to take orders from anyone. But an hour or so later he was bugging the shit out of himself with his foul mood.

It was late and dark, the ship quiet as most of the crew was either in bed, speaking on the phone to their families or crowded around one of the tables playing poker. Jackson stalked onto the empty deck and headed to the back of the ship. He tried not to glance over at *Emily's Fortune*. He didn't care what Loralei was doing.

Forcing his gaze away, he found himself standing in front of one of the launches. He just needed...some distance.

Lowering the smaller boat to the water, Jackson climbed in and headed for the island rising up in the distance.

It didn't take him long to reach the sandy shore. According to his research, this small stretch of land had been mostly uninhabited, used by fishermen and pirates over the years, but too small to sustain any real development.

But for now, it was perfect. He craved the solitude.

Taking the battery-powered lantern—standard issue for every launch boat—he headed out to explore, staying within the tree line close to shore.

The soft lap of the water against the sand moved with a cadence that tugged against him deep inside. The quiet, deserted night folded in around him, and, slowly, the restlessness that had been eating at him dissipated.

The blazing heat of the day had settled down to a pleasant mugginess that clung to his skin. The untamed riot of vegetation pressed in around him, making him feel more isolated from everything and everyone.

Stopping, Jackson stared up into the feathery canopy of leaves overhead. Moonlight was already streaming through and he could just make out a smattering of stars.

That's what he loved about being on the open water— no big cities and blazing lights to blot out the heavens. It always made him feel so small and at the same time profoundly immense.

He'd experienced the same thing in some of the more remote locations he'd traveled to with the Teams. Those moments had been unexpected gifts, finding a sense of peace in the middle of a shit-storm was often difficult.

Staring up at the stars always reminded him of his dad. It was something they'd shared, especially in the difficult year after his mother had left.

Anytime his father had sensed him struggling, he would pull out the secondhand telescope he'd scrounged up from somewhere and take Jackson outside to stare up at the heavens. He could still remember the soft murmur of his father's voice as he talked about the constellations and stories that went with them.

His dad had tried to hide his own devastation, tried to focus on Jackson and be what his son needed. But even at five, Jackson had recognized his father's pain. Resented his mother more because of it.

He'd never understood how a woman could walk away from a man who loved her that much, or how a mother could walk away from her only child.

In the end, his father and stepmother had found each other, which was better for everyone. But at the time...the experience had scarred and shaped him.

Not something he wanted to think about tonight. He had enough issues to deal with in the here-and-now.

With some perspective, it was easier to let the disappointment of the day melt away. So Loralei's crew had made the first find. That didn't mean they'd make the last. That was going to Trident's team. He'd worked too damn hard for anything else.

It would be easy to hope that the cannon wasn't from the *Chimera*. But it actually would mean more for him if it was.

It would mean they were on the right trail.

Dropping to the sandy ground, Jackson pressed his back

against the trunk of a tree. He extinguished the lantern he'd brought, to better see the night unfolding around him.

He'd just stay here for a bit before heading back.

BETWEEN THE ROCKING ship and the ball of excitement churning in her stomach, Loralei couldn't settle. Each tiny shift of the *Emily* had her heart thumping erratically.

She desperately wanted off. It was an itchy panic that settled right between her shoulder blades. She'd tried to talk herself out of the sensation, but it wasn't doing any good. In fact, the more she thought about where she was and what she was doing, the worse it became.

During the day, she'd been busy, her mind occupied. That was what she'd needed. If she wasn't going to get any sleep, she should probably just go back to her laptop and log a few more hours of research.

She was in the hallway headed back to the office when Brian popped out of the room in front of her.

"Great. I was just coming to look for you."

He snagged her elbow and propelled her in the opposite direction.

With a sigh, Loralei looked longingly back at the room that had been so close. "Why?"

"There are just a couple things we should go over before tomorrow's dive."

And they had to discuss them on deck? Loralei wanted to ask, but she knew if she voiced the words aloud Brian would wonder why it mattered.

So she swallowed them, and the familiar unease, to follow him up. He didn't stop until they were leaning against the railing, black water stretched out beside them.

Breathe. I'm fine. Safe on deck. Loralei forcibly dragged her gaze away, searched for something—anything—else to focus on.

The island.

In the distance she could make out the oasis of relief. Solid ground, trees spiking up several feet from the line of beach.

God, what she wouldn't give to be there right now instead of on the damn ship.

She could practically feel her feet sinking into the soft sand.

"So, tomorrow I'd like to dive farther out from the island," Brian said. His protests from the morning were now completely gone. It was amazing how finding the cannon had changed his attitude about her decision to come to the inlet.

Loralei tried not to be bitter about that, but it was difficult.

She looked at Brian and then at the island again. Maybe he'd be willing to take her over there. Although, then she'd have to explain why she was desperate to go explore an empty Caribbean island in the dark. And the thought of being there alone with him didn't sit well with her.

They had a small boat the crew used. As part of the standard safety briefing, Brian had given her a quick lesson when she'd come aboard.

Her salvation was so close. For the first time, Loralei understood how a man dying of thirst in the desert could convince himself sand was water. She wanted the relief. It was right there, yet...

With her gaze focused on the island, Loralei jerked when a shadow glided into her line of sight. No, not a shadow. A boat. With a single man.

She watched as the boat bumped up onto the sand. The man alighted, moving with a fluid, compact grace that she instinctively recognized.

Jackson Duchane was on that island.

In the middle of the night. Alone.

Why?

"Loralei, are you listening to me?" Brian asked.

She nodded, unwilling to pull her gaze away from Jackson. What was the man up to?

No good, that was the obvious answer.

He tied off the boat, grabbed something from beneath one of the seats and slipped silently into the tree line.

His movements were suspicious, which only increased her desire to unlock his motives and secrets. Did he suspect the island might hold more clues to the *Chimera*'s location?

That was the only logical reason she could think of for him to be out there in the dark. No matter what, she couldn't let him get to the lost ship ahead of her.

Someone below deck called for Brian. He gave her a hard look and then disappeared.

Loralei walked down the side of the ship, completely oblivious that the fear she'd been fighting not five minutes ago had dissipated.

Before she realized what she was doing, she'd climbed into the boat they kept tethered to the ship. She maneuvered the controls, just as Brian had taught her, and headed straight for where she'd seen Jackson disappear.

7

IT DIDN'T TAKE her long to cross the water, five minutes at most. About halfway across the panic hit again, full force. But at that point she was just as close to the island as she was to the *Emily*. She pulled alongside Jackson's boat, grabbed a rope and tied her own off as he'd done.

The euphoria that rushed through her the minute her feet touched the ground was unbelievable, but short-lived.

She didn't have time to luxuriate. She needed to find Jackson and figure out just what had drawn him here in the dark of night.

Grabbing a flashlight stashed in the boat, Loralei flicked it on and picked her way into the thick underbrush. There was little sound. The island was so small. She'd read that the only animals it could sustain were birds and smaller rodents.

Occasionally she heard a caw or chatter, but for the most part the island was silent. Part of her had been hoping for some sound that would lead her straight to him.

The stars were so bright out here in the middle of nowhere. Looking up, Loralei marveled at them. She'd seen stars before. She and Melody had even sat out on the roof of their first apartment building one summer night and stared up at them, laughing, talking and drinking cheap tequila until they'd both been cross-eyed drunk.

That night she'd thought the stars were so close. But compared to now it had been as if they'd been put on a dimmer switch and permanently turned to the lowest setting.

Forcing her gaze back in front of her, she trained her light on the ground and slowly moved forward. The beam was bright, but not bright enough to illuminate everything around her. And the farther she moved from the beach, the more the night seemed to press in.

Maybe this is a bad idea.

Loralei wondered where that voice of reason had been five minutes ago when she'd obviously needed it.

She was mentally arguing with herself when she stumbled over something. Her body pitched forward, her arms windmilled, desperate to regain her balance even as her brain told her it was a lost cause.

She sprawled inelegantly on the ground, cushioned by the layer of peaty-smelling leaves and debris. Her flashlight skittered and rolled before winking out completely. Without looking, she kicked out at what she assumed was the tree root that had tripped her. "Damn tree."

What she didn't expect was for the root to respond with a resounding, *"Ooomph."*

Letting out a startled squeak, Loralei scrambled back away from the sound. Her eyes were desperately trying to adjust, but unable to do it fast enough for her panicked brain.

Hands clamped around her upper arms, halting her.

"Loralei, stop."

She recognized that low, gruff voice. Her body immediately relaxed, even without the order from her brain.

"Jackson," she said. His name rolled off her tongue way too easily.

She heard a click and then light flared between them. It gilded his face, highlighting the sharp angles of his cheekbones and making his blue eyes flare.

"What are you doing out here?" he asked.

She shifted, unwilling to admit that she'd followed him…and then literally stumbled across him.

"I could ask the same of you," she countered to hide the guilt she had absolutely no reason to feel.

His eyebrows crinkled together as a reluctant smile tugged at his lips. Shaking his head, he let her go, and turned to search through the brush until he came up with her flashlight grasped tight in his fist.

Loralei snatched the light he held out to her and spun on her heel. She was several steps away when his silky voice reached out through the darkness and melted down her spine.

"Running away?"

Her feet faltered, kicking up sand as she stumbled to a stop.

"I'm not," she said, her words far from the forceful denial she'd intended.

"Aren't you? If I hadn't seen the real panic on your face, I'd almost think you'd masterminded the entire drowning episode last night just so you could get access to my research."

Anger buzzed through Loralei's head so loud it drowned out the incessant rush of the ocean pulling against the sand. Before she registered what she intended, Loralei was stalking toward him. "I am not a thief." She spat out the words like projectiles. "I didn't take anything from you."

Instead of standing his ground, Jackson moved backward, allowing her momentum to push them both until his back settled against the solid trunk of the tree he'd been using as a prop.

Uncaring—or unaware—of the situation she'd just launched herself in to, Loralei buried a single, accusing finger in the center of his chest and glared up at him.

Wrapping a hand around her wrist, Jackson tugged, reversing their positions until she was the one with her back against the rough bark.

His palms flattened on the trunk behind her, but he didn't touch her. He didn't have to. His entire body caged her in as effectively as any bars could have. Oh, she had the ability to duck under and escape, but her body just wouldn't obey the command. So she was stuck, staring into those damn gorgeous eyes that glittered down at her with a mixture of exasperation, anger and bone-deep lust.

God, she understood.

Her own emotions where this man was concerned were a tangle of contradiction and frustration.

She didn't want to want him, but apparently that didn't matter.

"What do you want from me, Loralei?"

"Nothing," she bit out, wanting desperately to mean it.

His thumb shifted, brushed lightly down the curve of her throat. A thrill raced through her, chased by goose bumps across her skin. A satisfied smirk tugged at the edges of his lips. Damn the man. He knew exactly what he was doing to her and enjoyed the power her response gave him.

"The least you can do is admit it. We both know the truth."

God, she hated this. He wasn't wrong and it bothered her to want or need anything from anyone. Her entire life she'd been alone. Preferred it that way.

She'd been fairly young when she'd realized she

couldn't depend on her parents for anything. Her father's work had always come first, no matter what. And even when her mother had been alive, her heart and soul had been out on the water not with her daughter.

Loralei's life was solitary, and that was the way she liked it. She'd never had a problem walking away from anyone or anything.

Although she knew she should, she couldn't seem to do that with Jackson. Despite her better judgment, he kept pulling her back in.

"Why are you on this island, Loralei, and not snuggled up in your warm bed on the ship?"

"I was restless," she said, shifting her gaze away from his too intense, too observant study. She didn't want him to read the rest of the reason, that she'd been drawn here by him.

Yes, because she'd needed to know what he was up to.

But also for this.

The way he made her body come alive just by pressing close. The way he made her want something she knew she couldn't have.

The way he made her feel vibrant and energized for the first time in…a very long time. It was an addiction she couldn't seem to shake. One she'd developed way too quickly. A couple of tastes and her willpower was toast.

It was the same buzz she got whenever she uncovered that kernel of information she'd been hunting days, weeks or sometimes months for.

Euphoria, triumph and anticipation.

Pressing his face close to hers, Jackson snagged her gaze and wouldn't let it go. He drilled her with those clear blue eyes, the ones she could drown inside without a hint of panic. "We both know you're scared to death of the water. So what really got you on that tiny boat and over to this little island?"

Unexpected heat rolled through her. Embarrassment. She didn't often get embarrassed and didn't appreciate that this man had the ability to set her off-kilter enough to manage it.

"I…" She wanted to lie, but for some reason the words wouldn't work through her throat. Not until they carried the truth. "I saw you."

The ghost of a smile tugged at his lips. Something hot and primitive flashed deep inside his eyes.

"So you followed me out here? Despite your debilitating fear?"

Another wave of the uncomfortable emotion swept through her. He was making her examine her own actions and motives, and she didn't particularly want to do that.

A single finger slipped down the slope of her heated cheek. "Yes," she admitted, the word dragging from deep inside without her permission.

"Why?"

She clamped her jaw shut rather than let out any more of her secrets. Loralei decided the smarter thing to do was to stay silent. Turning her head, she trained her gaze on the darkness surrounding them.

But Jackson was having none of that. With gentle pressure, he forced her to meet his eyes.

"Why, Loralei?" But then he surprised her by changing the question. "Why are you afraid of the water?"

Slowly, he pressed closer, taking what space had been between them and shrinking it down to nothing. "How did the daughter of a scuba diver end up unable to swim and afraid of the water?"

Loralei swallowed. She couldn't breathe, not with his body invading her space and his soft, insistent voice permeating her thoughts. She didn't mean for the words to slip out—they just did. "My mother drowned."

The simple statement was so much easier to say than she'd expected, but the feelings behind it were so much more complex. And Jackson seemed to sense that.

He touched her again. Not with the searing passion she wanted—that emotion would have helped her forget the things she didn't want to remember—but with soft, soothing caresses. His hands ran gently up and down her arms. His fingers paused at her shoulders to knead the tight muscles there. He coaxed her to relax, and her body was incapable of denying his talented, silent demand.

"I'm so sorry," he whispered, the words just as tempting. "How did it happen?"

For some strange reason she found herself answering, giving in to the gentle command that lurked behind the innocuous question. It was the soft sympathy she didn't want to want.

"I wasn't always afraid of the water," she explained.

Until she'd turned five, she'd lived on the *Emily* with both of her parents. She didn't have memories of those times, but there were pictures. Not that she looked at them often. But when she did, they all seemed so happy.

Then she and her mother had moved in with her grandparents. Water hadn't been the center of her world, but it had still been a part of her life. She'd gone to the pool, her hair in pigtails and sunscreen slathered all over her skin.

"I was nine when my mom left me to join my dad on a dive. Even that young, I knew she was restless. She got that way sometimes. She never said it to me personally, but I knew. She loved me, but there was a part of her that resented having to stay behind while my dad was diving at some of the most beautiful places on earth.

"Occasionally she'd leave me with my grandparents,

go off for a couple weeks whenever that urge to be on the water welled up and got really bad."

Instinctively, Loralei reached out for him, curling her fingers around his biceps and holding on tight.

"I remember the moment they told me. It's so crystal clear. Sometimes I wish it wasn't. That, like other childhood memories, it would fade. But it doesn't. I was at school. The principal came and got me out of class. I knew right then something bad must have happened. That terrible knot in my stomach only got worse when I saw my grandparents standing in the hallway. My grandmother's eyes were rimmed red and my grandfather just stood there, staring down at me with grief and pity in his eyes. They told me there'd been an accident and that my mom was gone. That she'd drowned."

Loralei closed her eyes, the emotions of that day overwhelming her all over again. The way her chest had tightened so much that she'd felt as if *she* was the one suffocating.

"The water was her life. She was one of the strongest swimmers I've ever known. And she drowned. How is that possible?"

Loralei's entire world spun again, just as it had that day so long ago when she'd learned what had happened. But in the middle of it, tonight, two solid hands were holding her up.

Jackson, maybe sensing that there was no good answer to her question, simply held on to her, giving her what she needed at that moment.

Memories rushed at her, overwhelming grief. The funeral had been a blur of people flowing in and out of their house. Everyone speaking in hushed voices. People she'd never met before patting her on the head as if she was a dog instead of a girl who'd just lost her mother.

For weeks she'd woken up every night covered in sweat, tears streaming silently down her face. She never told her grandparents about the nightmares where she imagined the cold, wet darkness slowly crushing and choking her mother. They had been dealing with their own grief. And she'd had to be strong, just like her father had told her to be before he'd left again.

"You've been afraid ever since." Jackson didn't ask, he knew. Understood.

"There's something about it that just…paralyzes me." The moment she touched pools, lakes or the ocean it was as if her arms and legs were filled suddenly with concrete. The familiar sensation of helplessness washed over her. God, she hated that.

A band tightened around her lungs, making it hard to pull in a full breath. Her heart sped up, thumping uncomfortably against every pulse point in her body. All of her—blood, bone, skin and muscle—went ice cold.

"Hey, hey," he said. Suddenly Jackson's warm hands cupped her cheeks. He tilted up her face until she was staring straight into eyes so deep and blue they should have reminded her of exactly what scared her to death.

Instead, Loralei felt a rush of unbelievable calm cascade over her. Her hands wrapped hard around his wrists, she held on.

They stared at each other for several moments, breathing in sync, in and out as the familiar panic drained away.

And still, he stared at her, steady and sure in a way nothing in her life had ever felt. She had no idea what Jackson was seeing, but her body started to respond differently, no longer ruled by remembered fear.

His thumb brushed across her lower lip, making it tingle.

She wanted him to kiss her. Hard and slow. To bring

that simmer in her blood up to a boil and take away everything else.

Which was why she pulled away.

She tried to sidestep out of his arms, but he refused to let her pass. She expected him to try to push the moment into a replay of the frenzy from the night before, so she was left off-kilter by the low rumble of Jackson's words.

"I understand, Loralei. I lost my mother, too."

8

JACKSON HAD NO idea why he'd told her this. Maybe it was the salt air or the moonlight or the way pain had welled up behind her gorgeous green eyes.

The sight of it had left a pit in the bottom of his stomach. He'd wanted to make that pain go away.

He'd always been that way, unable to handle seeing women upset. Yet another reason he didn't do relationships.

"She died?" Loralei's voice was husky, tinged with the emotions still swirling inside her.

Slowly, Jackson shook his head. No, his mother hadn't died. Was it bad that there'd been a time in his life when he'd wished she had? When he was fourteen he'd even told several of the guys at school that was what had happened.

It'd been easier to deal with their platitudes over his loss than their pity if he'd told them the truth.

"No. She left when I was five. Just…left. One day she dropped me off at kindergarten. That afternoon she was supposed to pick me up again, but my dad was waiting outside instead. He took me to get some ice cream."

"Why do adults always think ice cream will help kids deal with bad news?"

Jackson chuckled, appreciating her ability to make him smile in the middle of remembering one of the most painful moments of his life. "I have no idea, but it really doesn't help."

"At all."

"He explained that my mom was dealing with some things and for a while it was just going to be us boys. I'm not sure exactly when I realized she was never coming back. Not at Christmas a couple months later, even though she didn't call or send a card or anything. Maybe it was my birthday in May when my dad arranged to take all the boys from my class to a baseball game, but she wasn't there."

"Jackson," Loralei breathed.

"Don't you dare," he growled. "Don't you feel sorry for me."

That wasn't what he wanted. Ever.

"I'm not the first child to be abandoned. I was lucky. That first year was tough—for both of us—but I have the best dad and a wonderful woman I consider my mother. She came into my life about a year later. Made my dad happy again and gave me the best little sister, even if she was a pain in the ass on occasion growing up."

Loralei choked on a strangled laugh. "I always wanted a sister."

"God save me if you and Kennedy ever meet." He could just see it now, both of them terrorizing everyone, demanding and dictatorial.

"I didn't tell you that to gain sympathy. But to let you know I understand both the pain of losing a parent and the turmoil of being abandoned. Of growing up thinking there was something wrong with you because they chose something else over you."

Loralei sucked in a sharp breath. "I didn't… I don't…"

Her jaw snapped shut, locking whatever words she couldn't say behind tight teeth.

This time when Loralei moved to slip away he let her go. He turned to watch the sway of her hips, the long expanse of tanned legs and the tight swell of her ass against the tiny shorts she wore.

His body reacted. He wanted her. What red-blooded man wouldn't? But it was more than the simple lust he'd been fighting from the moment he'd seen her walking across the dock toward *Emily's Fortune*.

Dammit, why had he started this conversation? He really didn't want to understand any more about Loralei Lancaster. All he needed to know was that she was after the treasure he'd devoted his life to finding.

Which was why he wanted to smack himself when he hollered after her, "Do you want to learn?"

Loralei paused, only turning back enough to glance at him over her shoulder.

"What do you mean?"

"Do you want to learn how to swim?"

She was shaking her head before he could finish the sentence. "I already know how. I just…can't."

Taking several steps closer, Jackson was struck by how he was drawn to her despite himself. He knew he should keep his mouth shut and watch her walk away. But he couldn't seem to make himself do it.

"Oh, I think you can. Actually, I know you can. The woman I met the other night, the one who stared down an asshole at the bar and then dumped a drink over my head wouldn't let a little, insignificant thing like fear win."

"I've tried."

"Not with me."

Loralei let out a huff. "Arrogant, aren't you?"

Jackson couldn't stop a cocky grin from spreading

across his face or the dismissive shrug of his shoulders. "Sweetheart, you have no idea. I am a SEAL."

He took another step closer and with the decrease in distance could clearly see the fear swirling beneath her cool, calm facade. It bothered him for reasons he didn't particularly want to examine too closely.

"I won't let anything happen to you, Loralei. I worked too hard to revive your ass the first time."

She frowned, but the spark of temper had the advantage of dispelling at least some of her fear.

"Don't be a coward."

And that managed to take care of the rest.

Temper snapped, brightening her eyes. Her skin flushed and her body went stiff with indignation.

"I'm no coward. I'm here, aren't I?" Her arms waved around, taking in the expanse of water that stretched out in front of them.

"No, you're on this nice, solid island while the rest of your team is sound asleep on that ship behind you."

"Asshole," she breathed out.

"I heard that."

"Good."

A grin flashed across his lips.

"Are you going to let me try to help you or what? You know you want to. It can't be easy trying to hide your secret from your crew."

Dismay filled her features. "How'd you know…?"

"A hunch."

Loralei wasn't the kind of woman to admit to a weakness, not without being forced into a corner. She hadn't told him the truth until he'd been holding her out over the water and she'd been certain there was no other way to convince him to put her down. And even then, staring the real possibility of death in the face, the words had been reluctantly dragged through her lips.

Her eyes narrowed. "Why are you doing this?"

Now that was a damn good question. Jackson had no freaking clue. But since he'd already made the offer...

"Let's just say the idea of anyone being afraid of the water bothers me. Especially now that I know where your fear comes from. I've been diving for almost half my life. It's..." There were so many ways he could finish that sentence. "Everything. Let me help you."

Loralei cocked her head to the side and studied him for several moments before nodding slowly. "Fine. But don't blame me when this doesn't go well."

Oh, he wouldn't. He knew precisely where to place that blame. Squarely on his own shoulders.

"Tomorrow night. Right here, about nine."

Loralei nodded and then spun on her heel, kicking up sand as she jogged toward the small boat she'd left tied to a tree next to his.

He watched her crank the motor and head back to the ship anchored in the distance, keeping an eye on her the entire way.

ALL DAY SHE'D flip-flopped between dread, anger and unfortunately, lust. She'd been back on the *Emily* for about an hour before she'd realized Jackson hadn't actually answered her question. She still had no idea why he'd gone out to that island.

And now she really wanted to know. The curiosity was killing her. Right along with the sickening sludge of panic she didn't want to admit feeling.

It had been hard to concentrate on the tasks at hand. Her team had gone down again today, searching for more artifacts but coming up empty.

Once again, Loralei had spent the day below deck working on her research.

Several times she'd convinced herself that she wasn't going to do it. She'd be stupid to follow through and meet Jackson on that beach. But then she'd hear his voice, low and gruff, accusing her of being a coward.

And she was. She'd been a coward for almost her entire life. At least where water was concerned. It bothered her, imagining Jackson smirking at her, thinking he'd pegged her perfectly.

He didn't know anything about her.

Which was how she found herself on that damn tiny launch, headed for the sandy shore. Beneath the cutoff jean shorts and T-shirt she'd thrown on, she wore a bathing suit. It was a rather optimistic move, but she'd put it on anyway.

It was the first one she'd bought in a very long time. As a teenager, she'd bought swimsuits so that she could visit the pool with her friends, although the only time they'd gotten wet was when she washed them.

This was the first time she'd had this one on outside the dressing room. The tight strings that tied around her neck and ribs rubbed uncomfortably. Or maybe it was the stress and fear that made her uncomfortable. Her nerves buzzed with tension, making her feel as if her entire body was conducting a live current.

As she steered the boat up on the beach she looked for Jackson's, but couldn't find it. Maybe *he'd* changed his mind. That thought had relief and anger coursing through her. She resented both emotions.

Climbing out of the boat, Loralei tied it off to a nearby tree and scanned the dense jungle. Well, if she wasn't going to have to deal with her fear tonight, at least she'd get some time with her feet on solid ground again.

Tucking her hands into her pockets, she strolled for the

line of vegetation and nearly gasped when Jackson materialized out of the gathering gloom.

"You came."

Loralei frowned. Did he think she wouldn't?

"I said I would."

Quirking a single eyebrow, Jackson said, "I wasn't sure that actually meant something to you."

"If you really think that little of me, why are you doing this?"

Jackson shook his head. "I already told you. Strip."

It was her turn to raise an eyebrow. "Excuse me?"

His lips twitched. "You better have something on under those clothes that you don't mind getting wet. Strip." He spun his finger around in the air in the universal sign for hurry it up.

Immediately, Loralei's back went up. Her fingers snapped to the fly of her shorts and tore at the button and zipper. With a jerky roll of her hips, her shorts dropped to the sand at her feet. Grasping the hem of her shirt, she whipped it over her head and tossed it at him.

The bastard ducked, snatched the soft cotton out of the air and slung it around his shoulders as if that was precisely where he'd wanted it in the first place.

His eyes took a leisurely tour of her body. Loralei became acutely aware of just how much her suit revealed. Not that she'd ever been the kind of woman to care. Before tonight. She was comfortable in her own skin, or always had been.

And, hell, he'd seen more of her the other night.

Something about the way Jackson looked at her made every molecule in her body respond, desperate for the feel of his hands on her again.

But that wasn't what tonight was about.

Shaking away her reaction, Loralei cocked a hip and crossed her arms over her chest.

Unfortunately, she'd apparently miscalculated, because instead of having the desired effect of putting him in his place, it only made the heat in his eyes kindle higher.

Stepping closer, Jackson crowded into her personal space. His hands wrapped around her upper arms, spun her until her body was surrounded by his heat.

Back to front, his thighs bracketed hers. Her rear settled into the cradle of his hips. She could feel his strength, not just behind her, but soaking straight through her skin and permeating her bones. Nudging her knees with his, he walked slowly, pushing her in front of him, until the gentle lap of the water touched her toes.

Suddenly, Loralei couldn't have cared less who was holding her. The only thing that mattered was the water in front of her. Sure it was clear and shallow at her feet, but a little ways out…it was so deep it could swallow her whole. Suck her under and consume her.

Tension wound every muscle in her body so tight she was afraid they would all snap and she would lose it. Just… lose it.

That was the last thing she wanted to do in front of this man. Again. She'd already experienced enough humiliation in his presence to last her a lifetime.

Yet, she couldn't stop it.

The panic welled up, filled her chest and stomach and head. Her lungs burned.

Something soft brushed her ear. And a commanding voice murmured, "Breathe, Loralei."

Until that moment she hadn't been aware that she wasn't. But the second Jackson issued the demand, her mouth opened, her lungs expanded and blessed oxygen flooded her cells.

That first draw was heaven, her chest rising and her back arching beneath the weight of the relief and release that came with the exhale.

"Close your eyes," he whispered against her skin. His breath was warm and soothing. But Loralei shook her head anyway.

"Close. Your. Eyes."

Before she realized what she was doing, her eyelids were slipping shut.

"I have you. Nothing is going to happen to you. I promise. You're safe."

It had been so long since anyone had said that to her. Not her grandparents. Not her father.

She wanted to believe Jackson meant it. They might be rivals on those ships anchored not far away, but tonight he was more friend than enemy. And instinctively she knew that no matter what else was between them, he wouldn't let anything happen to her.

Slowly, he nudged one foot and then the other. She could feel the water lap first at her toes, then ankles, then calves.

She began to tremble, slight tremors she couldn't control no matter how hard she tightened her muscles. Her entire body ached with the force of trying to will away the panic. It wasn't working.

"That's it. You're doing great."

When the water hit just above her knees, Jackson said, "Open your eyes."

He'd guided her out around a small bend she hadn't noticed when she'd drove the boat in. Sand and dense vegetation surrounded them on three sides. In front of them the ocean spread out, sparkling beneath the rising moon. She couldn't see their ships in the distance anymore. The small cove was protected. Secret.

Just theirs.

It was beautiful. Calm and peaceful. Loralei stood surrounded by Jackson's heat and support, and tried to let that peace wash over her. It didn't quite work.

He let her stand there, not pushing or impatient, and waited for some innate sign that she was ready to take the next step.

Loralei had no idea how long they stayed like that in silence, but eventually Jackson dropped a hand to her hip and nudged her forward. Her feet shuffled against the sandy floor. His fingers branded her through the thin material of her bathing suit. Her body reacted, going liquid and warm. Which was probably why she didn't notice the water rising steadily up her legs until it hit midthigh.

Distraction. Apparently, that was his tactic. And it was working. She hadn't been this deep in water without hyperventilating since she was nine.

"How're you doing?" he asked, the rough timber of his voice rippling through her.

She nodded, afraid to trust her voice.

Jackson shook his head. She felt the motion, his upper body shifting against her and sending delicious waves of sensation across her skin. "I need words, Loralei. You have to talk to me so I know you're okay."

"What if I don't want to talk to you?"

"Tough," he said, his voice warm with suppressed laughter.

"Fine," she huffed. "I'm…okay." And she was, which surprised the hell out of her.

"Excellent," he said before scooping up a handful of water and flinging it at her.

Loralei gasped in surprise, jerked forward and threw her elbow back.

Jackson grunted when she landed a hit straight to his

middle. He doubled over, bent her with him and somehow managed to submerge her shoulders deep into the water at the same time.

Every molecule of air rushed from her lungs as if they'd collapsed. Her mouth opened and her lips moved, but nothing came in or out.

Anticipating her reaction, Jackson was right there. Grasping her face, he brought them nose to nose, forcing her to look at him and nothing else.

"You're fine, Loralei. I have you. I promise. Breathe."

Her lungs obeyed him, expanding and filling on a huge gulp.

When she could speak again, she wheezed out, "You bastard."

He just grinned at her. "You're in, aren't you?"

She was. Fully submerged up to her collarbones with the water lapping gently at the curve of her throat.

But she wasn't about to admit that to him.

"You going to hold my head under the water next?" she groused and glared at him, which was difficult when he was busy staring at her through those twinkling, mischievous eyes.

"I wouldn't do that," he said, his words filled with mock sincerity.

"Yeah, right."

Her doubt seemed to sober him. The smirk slipped from his lips and his fingers tightened around her shoulders. "I wouldn't, Loralei. This was like ripping a Band-Aid off all at once. It hurts like hell and leaves you breathless, but it's ultimately the best method. Forcing your head under water is another thing all together."

Loralei wanted to believe him. She honestly did. But part of her just…couldn't. Not yet anyway.

As if sensing he shouldn't push her on the subject, Jackson asked, "How's the water?"

For the first time, Loralei realized it was… "Amazing." It was perfect against her suddenly overheated skin.

Jackson held her that way, his strong arms wrapped around her shoulders, his legs entwined with hers beneath the surface of the water. And she marveled at how comfortable she felt with him. Maybe it was the fact that this man was probably the first person she'd ever been completely honest with about her fear. Or maybe it was just him, transferring that sense of calm and ease in the water that came from years of experience and practice. Whatever it was, Loralei was grateful for the gift.

Even if it was coming to her from him.

"Ready to try more?"

Loralei hesitated. "What did you have in mind?"

"I won't push you in, but you will have to put your head under the water."

An uncomfortable knot pulled hard and tight in her belly. The familiar anxiety spun up, engulfed her entire body. There was no way Jackson could miss the sudden way every muscle stiffened.

But he didn't push. Instead, he ran comforting hands to the nape of her neck and dug his thumbs into the divot there, releasing the pressure and tension.

"How about we do it together?"

"How do you propose to do that?"

One corner of his lips turned up, not in that cocky grin or mischievous smirk she'd come to expect, but with something more. Heat, promise, some impish fun.

"Like this."

Before she could blink, he brought their mouths together. The kiss surprised her. It was different from the ones they'd shared before. Oh, there was sizzle, but beneath it, something soothing.

He immediately pulled her into the moment, nibbling, coaxing, until he was all she could think of. His tongue licked across her lips, requesting entrance. It didn't occur to her to refuse.

Hers parted and his tongue plunged inside, sweeping and claiming. His fingers tightened in her hair and she arched closer against the solid warmth of his body.

Pulling back, he whispered, "Take a deep breath." He sealed their mouths together again after she complied and then slowly pulled them under.

Cool water flowed over her, but instead of making her panic, it relieved some of the heat and pressure. It felt good against her over-sensitized skin.

They were only down a few seconds, not nearly enough time for her brain to process fully, before he was pushing them back up again. And pulling away, a wary look in his eyes as if he expected her to deck him.

Maybe she should.

But her fingers and arms wouldn't have obeyed her even if she'd wanted to.

She was panting, but not from fear.

His thumb brushed across her wet cheeks, sweeping away droplets of water. That simple, single caress had her knees buckling. Without his arm around her she would have collapsed back into the water.

"Easy," he said, the vibration of the word rolling through her chest.

Loralei blinked, trying to force her brain back into action. She should be upset. Why? Oh, yeah.

"Bastard," she whispered, the word holding absolutely none of the heat she'd intended.

Jackson's lips curved into that damn smirk. And all she wanted to do was kiss him again.

"I knew you could do it. Wanna try again? On your own this time?"

She did. She actually did. Loralei gave a small nod, but then followed it up with a bigger, more certain one, because if she was doing this, she was doing it. No half measures or second guessing.

"Good. Take a deep breath. And remember I've got you. I won't let anything happen to you."

Why was Jackson Duchane the first person in her life she'd ever believed when he uttered those words? It wasn't as if he'd done anything to earn her trust.

Maybe it was *because* he hadn't done anything to earn her trust. He'd been manipulative. Thrown her off a boat. Saved her life. Antagonized and accused.

What he hadn't done was pull any punches.

Filling her lungs with air, Loralei braced herself, let her legs fold underneath her and sank like a rock to the bottom of the sandy inlet.

Her butt bounced off the sea floor. Her mouth opened in surprise and water rushed in. Before she could panic or process, she was being hauled back up, air chasing after the water.

She sputtered for a second, too worried about breathing to notice she was tucked against Jackson's hard chest for a few moments.

And then it was all she could think about.

He had one arm behind her shoulders, the other beneath her knees. Her arms were tight around his neck. Water lapped against her, a gentle caress that made her think about his fingers sliding across her body, awakening every cell.

"Are you okay?"

Slowly, Loralei shook her head. Not even close.

9

Disgusted with himself, Jackson waded through the waist deep water toward the sandy shore. His jaw ached from clenching it tight.

Somehow he managed to push "I'm sorry," between his grinding teeth.

Loralei shifted in his arms, accidentally brushing the curve of her ass against his half-hard erection. He pulled in a sharp hiss.

Apparently she was oblivious to what she'd just done. "What are you sorry about? You didn't do anything wrong."

She squirmed again, shoving her fingers deeper into the hair at his nape and gripping tighter. If she didn't stop he was going to have two choices, drop her butt-first into the shallow water at their feet or lay her out across the soft sandy beach and finish what they'd started two nights ago.

He had a preference, but didn't think Loralei was in the right frame of mind for that.

Better if he kept his focus squarely where it belonged. "You weren't ready and I pushed you."

She frowned, tiny ridges forming between her gorgeous green eyes. Tonight they were darker than normal, or maybe that was just because of the moonlight.

"Not true."

Her breath puffed out, slipped across the skin of his neck. Moist warmth hit the cool droplets of water clinging to him and sent a bolt of need straight to his cock.

"Dammit," he cursed softly.

His grip, where his fingers curved into her hip, tightened. A few more steps. The moment his feet hit dry sand, he let her go. But that was a true miscalculation because instead of falling away, her body slithered down. Her breasts, barely contained by the tight Lycra of her suit, rubbed across his chest.

Her bare thighs brushed his hip. And her hands stayed clasped together behind his neck. The pressure made his back curve as her feet hit the ground.

They were centimeters apart. Her mouth was open. Inviting.

And he was a man who could only take so much.

Pulling her to him again, Jackson kissed her. This time there was no ulterior motive beneath the joining of their mouths. It was pure, unadulterated desire. Heat blasted through him. Loralei sighed, a soft puff of sound that caressed his lips.

Her leg lifted, wrapped around his waist and he was done. Gone. Any good intentions disappeared like so much smoke.

He tugged at the strings of her bikini top until the damn thing finally gave. It fell into the water that lapped at their ankles.

Somehow both of Loralei's legs found their way up his hips and around his waist. She climbed him, the entire time nipping, licking and sucking, her tongue stroking his.

Jackson wasn't complaining. At all. In fact, he let out a

deep groan when she squeezed her thighs and rubbed the cleft of her sex against his throbbing erection.

He could feel her heat through the thin layers of clothing separating them. Wanted desperately to sink deep inside her.

Loralei arched back, pulled her mouth from his. A breathy, desperate sound ground out of her throat. It was the sexiest thing he'd ever heard. And he wanted to make her do it again.

Reaching down, he sucked the dark pink tip of her breast into his mouth. Her breath hitched, the rough sound melting into something more when he scraped the edge of his teeth across the puckered flesh.

God, she tasted good. A combination of sunshine and the salty sea. He wove his fingers through her thick hair, letting the soft strands caress his skin.

He couldn't get enough of this woman.

Which was a problem. But one he'd search for a solution to later. Right now his brain couldn't concentrate on anything but experiencing her.

She writhed against him, arching her back and silently asking for more.

Dropping to his knees, he plunged them both into the shallow water. It surrounded them, warm and welcoming. Her dark hair fanned out around her head, floating in a sunburst.

Her skin was flushed, glowing with the same desire that radiated from him.

Her lips, already swollen, parted, begging for more. But she was far from acquiescent, not waiting for him to give her what she wanted. He'd hardly known her any time at all, but already recognized that wasn't Loralei.

Grasping his waistband, she went searching for the string tucked inside. The backs of her fingers grazed the hard length of his sex. Jackson sucked in a groan, his hips surging forward, wanting more.

A knowing smirk touched her lips and her eyes twinkled. God, she was gorgeous.

Her fingers intertwined with the string, pressing the rough edge of it against him and lazily dragging it across his swollen flesh.

Jackson fought the urge to brush her hands out of the way and untie his shorts himself, caught between the need climbing higher and the exquisite torture of her touch.

Slowly, she tugged on the braided cord, her other hand delving beneath his waistband to palm him. A groan welled up from deep inside his chest. He was so lost in the pleasure of her fist sliding up and down that he barely noticed his shorts splash into the water.

Rolling them both, Jackson set her on top, parting her thighs wide and settling them on either side of his hips. But she didn't let go. Her grip on his cock only tightened, her thumbnail scraping gently across the sensitive head. He hissed through his clenched teeth.

Grasping her hips, Jackson hooked his thumbs into her bikini bottoms, dragged them down her thighs. Somehow she managed to shift and shimmy until they were gone, all while continuing her slow, measured torment.

God, he wanted inside her. But he wanted to taste her first.

Flexing his hands, Jackson lifted her straight into the air. Dropping backward, he let the soft, sandy floor catch him even as he settled her thighs around his ears.

The scent of her arousal surrounded him, thick and heady. "Gorgeous," he growled before nuzzling her swollen flesh.

She was hot and wet. Sweet and salty. Perfect. Just like the whimper that fell from her parted lips.

Jackson swept his tongue over her, enjoying the way she pulsed and clenched, and begged him to plunge inside. Instead, he found the tiny bundle of nerves at the top and swirled around it, going so close, but never quite touching.

He tortured them both, his own body throbbing uncontrollably with every breathy sound and muffled moan. Loralei arched back, pushed her sex closer to his mouth, searching for relief he wasn't quite ready to give.

Her palms settled at his waist, her fingers digging in hard. Her hair brushed back and forth, a silken waterfall softly caressing his pounding erection. He was driving them both crazy.

And it felt so damn good. She felt so damn good.

Unable to deny himself what they both wanted any longer, Jackson plunged his tongue into the greedy opening of her sex. Loralei cried out, her entire body shuddering. Swirling a fingertip across her clit, Jackson reveled in the way she lost control.

Uninhibited, Loralei bucked against his mouth. The taste of her filled him. He needed more.

Jackson didn't even wait for her climax to end before shifting her onto her back. She settled in the soft sand and several inches of water. Her body was pliant and beautiful when he opened her thighs wide.

"I don't have a condom," he panted out.

Loralei laughed, the sound a thin tinkle that tripped across his senses. "I'm not sure whether to be angry or flattered. Nice to know you didn't bring me out here with the sole purpose of seducing me."

"Stop fishing for compliments. We both know I've wanted you from the minute I saw you."

"I'm on the pill and clean. The last lover I had was eighteen months ago."

"So am I. Just donated blood and was tested."

Loralei's answer was to spread her thighs wider, arch up and offer him everything. And Jackson accepted, plunging deep inside.

Her eyes went wide, a moan falling from her lips. Her sex rippled around him.

"Jesus, Loralei," he groaned, stilling. He had to find his sanity, not to mention some damn control. He didn't want to hurt her and he was so damn close to losing any sense of civility that he'd ever laid claim to.

She dug her fingers into his hips, rolling her own, urging him to move.

"Stop," he ground out. "Just…give me a minute."

Shaking her head, she stared up at him. He recognized the wide-eyed, lust-filled expression because he had no doubt he was wearing the same damn one.

He'd just made her scream and still she wanted more.

If this woman wasn't trying to rip him off, she'd be damn near perfect. Too perfect.

Shaking away the unwanted thought, Jackson began to move. Her sex squeezed him, the aftershocks of her release sizzling along his sensitive shaft. Quick and shallow, hard and deep, he could stay buried inside her welcoming heat forever.

But neither of them would last that long. At least not tonight.

When he could feel her entire body quivering, when she was whimpering mindless syllables that were probably supposed to be words, he finally let himself go.

The climax rolled up from the base of his spine, exploding out in a shower of unbelievable relief and pleasure. He groaned her name, only marginally appeased that his own name was echoing off the water surrounding them.

Slowly, they drifted back to earth.

Loralei shifted, her eyes cracking open to glittering

slits of deep emerald. A satisfied smile tugged at her lips and Jackson couldn't stop the intense feeling of pride and power at the knowledge that he'd put that sated, drowsy expression on her face.

"That was…nice."

"Nice, huh?" he murmured. "Pretty sure it was a hell of a lot more than that."

"Mmm." Her agreement buzzed against his skin.

At some point he'd stretched out beside her, his thigh and arm slung over her body. She stretched, arching languidly. Her breasts rose above the gently lapping water. For a second Jackson contemplated pulling one peak into his mouth again, but decided they both could use a few minutes before attempting round two.

Instead, he rose up, digging one elbow into the soft sand so he could look down at her.

Grabbing a handful of water, he trickled it over the part of her body exposed to the moonlight.

"Don't look now, but I'm pretty sure your fear of water is gone."

He watched her eyes pop wide and her body stiffen. But only for a few seconds. Her gaze jerked around them, taking in their private inlet, the stars twinkling above them and the water surrounding them.

Her chest rose and fell on a deep, heavy breath. The pulse at the base of her neck fluttered erratically for several seconds. He watched her fight the last fingers of fear as they tried to slip back through and claim her again.

Her jaw tightened and her eyes narrowed.

God, she was stubborn. He admired that about her. Not many people had the guts to face head on the kind of debilitating fear he'd witnessed.

Finally finding his gaze, she stared up at him for several seconds. Her hands played quietly through the water, swishing back and forth. A look of wonder dawned slowly across her face. It was one of the most dazzling things he'd ever seen.

Tears he never would have expected glittered at the corners of her eyes.

"Thank you," she whispered, the words thick and husky with emotion.

"I didn't do anything," Jackson argued. It had been all her. He'd just stood beside her to give her courage and support. She was the one who'd actually confronted her fear.

"You did more than you realize."

THE ADMISSION HAD been difficult to give, but true. She never could have gotten through those moments in the water without him.

That, more than anything, had her rolling away from him. Pushing to her feet, Loralei glanced around, looking for her bathing suit.

The thing had been rather bright with tropical flowers in red, yellow, orange and pink on a black background. Easy enough to spot even in the moonlight. Or it should have been.

Shallow water lapped at her ankles and a brief spurt of dread fired up in her belly.

Glancing out, Loralei saw a brief flash of pink caught in the up swell of a wave.

"You have got to be kidding me," she moaned.

But, no, if she thought about it logically, why wouldn't her bathing suit be drifting out to sea?

Because that was exactly how every encounter with Jackson Duchane seemed to end. Drinks over his head, near drownings and trips to the ER.

Still lounging in the water, Jackson pushed onto his elbows and gazed up at her.

"What?"

With a silent finger, she pointed toward the tiny speck of her suit in the distance.

Not even bothering to try not to splash, Loralei headed for the shore.

Suddenly, she felt naked. Oh, she'd been that way for a while, but she could feel the weight of Jackson's gaze as it traveled from her calves to her thighs and then to her ass.

She told herself not to, but she glanced behind her just in time to catch him wiping the water she'd splashed out of his face, even as he kept his eyes trained on her body. Lust suffused his every feature.

Something primitive inside her responded.

Which was precisely why she had to get away from him. They'd scratched an itch that had been irritating them both for the past couple days.

That's what had just happened and nothing more.

She wouldn't let it be anything more.

Jackson made her nervous and frustrated. Not to mention he left her shaky with need. Out of control. That was what he did. He pushed her and cajoled and finagled and somehow managed to override her instincts to protect herself.

Such as now. She was standing on the shore, staring, unable to pull her gaze away from the spectacle of him rising up to follow her.

His body was amazing, all toned muscle and barely banked strength. It took little imagination to consider him as a lethal weapon. But she'd never seen any evidence that he was inclined to use that honed skill.

Logically, she realized he must have at some point in his career. That realization should have made her wary. Instead, it made her want to wrap her arms around his body and hold him tight.

Which was damn funny considering Jackson Duchane was the least likely man she'd ever met to require comfort or an infusion of strength.

He was only a few steps away from her when Loralei managed to shake herself out of her stupor.

She darted for the shorts and shirt she'd left in a bundle on the sand. Reaching down, she shook them out as best she could.

Jackson's strong arm wrapped around her from behind, pulling her into his body.

"Where do you think you're going?"

"Back."

He bent down, running his mouth up the sensitive slope of her neck. Loralei tilted, unconsciously giving him more and offering herself, even as she tried to wrap her arms around her waist and cover herself.

"Why?"

"Because…" She needed to escape. To think. To get back to reality and sanity. "I should get back to my crew."

"The crew that don't know you're gone?"

"That won't last long. Someone's going to realize the launch is missing soon enough."

"Hmm." The sound vibrated into her skin.

The sensation was delicious and sent shivers rocking up and down her spine.

His fingers wandered, digging into her hip, finding the curve of her breast, brushing across her flesh in a caress that left her skin tingling.

How could she want more so soon?

Loralei jerked herself out of his arms. She had her shirt over her head in seconds flat. The maneuver she used to get her shorts on was hardly elegant, hopping from one foot to the other. But it accomplished what she needed.

Slowly, she backed away from him, inching toward her boat tied up farther down the shore.

A frown tugged at the edges of Jackson's mouth.

"You're really going to leave?"

"Yes." She was. Because she had to get away from him before she managed to lose every last shred of self-preservation.

The temptation to stay was strong. Strong enough to scare her. She didn't want to need anyone, least of all Jackson, for anything. Including physical pleasure.

But what they'd just shared had been light years ahead of any sexual encounter she'd ever had. Most women would think that a good thing. Loralei wasn't convinced.

Maybe it was just the animosity that ran under the surface between them.

Yeah, maybe that was it.

"You're just going to leave me here? Without any clothes? My trunks are in the middle of the ocean with your suit and I didn't bring anything else."

Something akin to drunken bliss bubbled up inside Loralei's chest, escaping as laughter. It was a good sensation.

Which was why she shook her head.

"Not my problem."

Without waiting for his response, she turned and sprinted for the boat.

Part of her expected him to come after her. To snatch her up and use his persuasive mouth and hands to convince her to stay.

But he didn't. When she looked back, he was watching her, arms crossed comfortably over his chest like some naked lord of the island. All the man was missing was a crown fashioned from dried sea grass and encrusted with shells to complete the picture. His bronzed skin gleamed in the moonlight. Tiny droplets of water still glistened in his sandy blond hair.

The entire ride back to the *Emily* that was all she could think about.

And she had no idea what kept her from turning around and going back.

10

OKAY, SO SHE wasn't *cured.*

Loralei stood at the railing that ran the length of the deck, staring out at the ocean, and fought down the wave of nausea that threatened to have her dropping to her knees.

She'd been fine, right up until the moment she'd leaned out and looked down.

Why hadn't the water bothered her last night? Was it just that she'd been so totally overwhelmed by Jackson's charismatic presence and her own libido?

Probably.

Not to mention the inlet had been fairly shallow. She didn't want to guess at the depth of the water the *Emily* was currently cutting through.

Around her, the crew scurried from one point to another, doing whatever they needed to direct the ship and prepare for their next diving location. Early in the morning, they'd headed out from the inlet, confident that the only artifact left there was already on board.

It hadn't escaped her notice that the *Amphitrite* had already been gone.

Apparently, it'd been Jackson's turn to leave before dawn.

Now why did that thought hurt?

Not that it would take them long to catch up.

What had happened last night had been a mistake. A result of her combined vulnerability and elation that never should have occurred. And wasn't going to happen again.

She and Jackson were water and oil. Or better yet, gasoline and a match, ready to flame up the moment they made contact.

She'd seen the way Jackson's eyes lit up any time he thought about the *Chimera*. The thrill of the chase. That's what it was. She'd seen that same fever in her father's eyes. Had resented it when he'd chosen the need for adventure over taking care of his frightened, grieving, lonely daughter.

The last thing she wanted was to fall for an unavailable man, someone who wouldn't be there for her when she needed him most.

"Loralei, are you okay?" Brian slipped up beside her, wrapping a hand around her arm and pulling her straight. "You don't look so hot. You aren't getting seasick, are you?"

His forehead wrinkled with worry. She hated to lie to him, but he'd offered her the perfect excuse and she'd be stupid not to take it.

"Maybe a little," she said. She didn't have to fake the grimace that accompanied the words.

"You didn't before."

"I did. I just didn't say anything."

"Well, that's silly. There are things you could do. I'm sure one of the guys has patches or those wristbands that work with pressure points."

Loralei let a sickly smile slip across her lips. "I thought it would pass once I got used to being on the open water. But, yeah, maybe that would help."

"Why don't you sit down over there while I ask around?"

Loralei started to protest, but Brian had her moving across the deck in the direction of a bench that was close by.

She tried not to lean into the comforting arm he wrapped around her waist. Or sigh with relief when the water was out of her line of sight and her stomach quit rolling. Okay, so she just couldn't look directly down at it.

With a hand on her shoulder, Brian urged her down onto the seat close to a huge tank of water bolted to a raised table. The entire thing was clear, giving her a perfect view of the artifact inside. Their conservation specialist had submerged the cannon in a bath of mostly freshwater mixed with a chemical to help wash away the salt. Without the treatment, the cannon would slowly crumble away to nothing once exposed to the air. Saltwater was not kind to metals.

The minute Loralei's eyes landed on the chipped and corroded metal resting inside, a thrill shot through her. Most people might not think of the cannon as beautiful—dingy with a crust of orange rust and barnacles after being submerged for 150 years—but it really was.

Or rather, the story it told and its connection to the past were beautiful.

"Is it the *Chimera*'s?" she asked, unable to keep the reverence and hope from her voice.

"Without a single doubt," Eric said.

Excitement welled up. Loralei leaned closer, wanting a better look at the artifact. From across the deck one of the hands hollered her name.

Waving the interruption away, Loralei yelled back, "Not now, Luis. I'll find you in a few minutes."

Turning her focus back to Eric, she raised a single eyebrow and silently asked him to finish.

The glee in his eyes said he was only too happy to oblige. "Do you see these markings?" Dropping into a crouch beside the tank, he pointed to a discolored patch of metal toward the thicker end of the cannon. "Each gun was stamped with identifying markings. They're often hard to make out, especially after over a hundred years in the water, but we were lucky. Your father found a manifest of everything aboard, including the weaponry. This cannon was listed."

Loralei couldn't stop the whoop of glee that flew past her lips. She jumped up so quickly the crown of her head collided with Brian's chin. She hadn't been aware he was standing that close to her.

Her exclamation of delight turned into a cry of pain. She grabbed her head and stumbled.

Even with a hand pressed to the lower half of his face, Brian's curses were clear enough that she got the gist. Several bright drops of blood seeped through his fingers.

Cursing, Loralei stepped closer and peeled his hand away so she could get a good look.

His nose didn't appear to be broken and already the blood had slowed to a trickle.

"I'm fine," Brian said, his voice muffled and slightly strained. With a grimace, he pushed Loralei's hand away from his face and wiped away the blood. But he didn't let her go.

Instead, he used their connection and her proximity to draw her closer. His other arm wrapped around her waist.

It wasn't the first time Brian had touched her, but something about the way he held her now made her feel uncomfortable. As if he was doing something wrong. Or she was, although she hadn't asked him to invade her personal space.

"We're close," he whispered into her ear. An unwanted and unpleasant shiver rocked her body. She tried to pull away, but he only let her put an inch or two between them.

Looking down at her, he smiled. "Your dad would be proud."

A tight band constricted her chest at the mention of her father. She could just imagine his excitement. And the thought of sharing this moment with him… It overwhelmed her. Made her throat ache and her chest tighten.

She pushed away her reaction. There was nothing much she could do with it—her father wasn't coming back and she'd never get the opportunity to share this piece of the *Chimera* with him, no matter how much she might wish for it.

Loralei forced more space between her and Brian.

For the first time she realized just how quiet the deck had gotten. It was eerie and unusual. With almost a dozen guys living and working on the ship, there was always noise.

Stepping back, Loralei let her gaze sweep across the deck and nearly swallowed her tongue when she reached the tall man with bright blue eyes glaring at her.

No, Jackson wasn't glaring at her. That dark, dangerous gaze was trained just over her shoulder. At Brian.

JACKSON'S HANDS TIGHTENED into hard balls. He was fighting the urge to stalk across the deck, slam a fist straight into Brian's face and wipe that smug smile off the asshole's lips.

The way he'd looked down at Loralei…it had set all sorts of warning bells clanging inside Jackson's head.

He knew a besotted fool when he saw one and there was

no doubt in his mind that Brian Peterson wanted Loralei. And probably had for as long as he'd known her.

His trigger finger itched for a weapon, something he hadn't wanted since the day he'd left the Teams. He'd had enough of bloodshed and killing.

The way Loralei jumped away from Brian, a look of guilt crossing her expressive face, didn't help.

He watched her gather her thoughts, her body following suit as she straightened her spine and pulled herself up to her full height.

With long, dark hair swirling around her shoulders, she paced forward, completely oblivious to the fact that half the men on deck watched her with hungry eyes.

He wanted to snatch her to him, bend her back and kiss the hell out of her. If for no other reason than to let every man watching—especially Brian—know that she was his.

But she wasn't.

And he'd never been the possessive type. Typically he was a "love and let love" kind of guy. He didn't like restrictions placed on his own movements, so he didn't place them on anyone he slept with.

Why, then, did he want to haul Loralei into the cabin and remind her exactly what they'd done last night?

"Jackson. What are you doing here?"

Why *was* he there? When he'd convinced himself to take the launch to *Emily's Fortune* so that he could persuade Loralei to let him have a look at the cannon the reasoning had sounded good in his head. But now…he realized it was a hell of a lie. Loralie had no incentive whatsoever to give him what he wanted.

If he was honest, what he'd really hoped for when he'd set off had been the chance to touch and kiss her again. It was all he'd been able to think about, even when he'd been working sixty feet under the surface of the water and should have been concentrating on his damn job.

"We need to talk," he said.

Several of the men surrounding them shuffled and shifted. Brian moved to step in front of Loralei, but she didn't seem to notice. Or care.

Cocking her head to the side, she drilled him with a knowing stare. "All right," she said, drawing out the two words. "Follow me."

She led him below deck, to a stateroom that was sparsely furnished, and ushered him inside. The door closed softly behind her. Jackson stopped in the center of the room and spun to face her.

Loralei lounged against the door, her hand lodged on the knob behind her back. Her hips jutted forward, feet spread wide in unconscious accommodation of the ship's constant swaying. For a woman who was afraid of the water, she'd adapted rather quickly to living on it. He wasn't sure if she was even aware of how naturally her body moved with the motion.

"No, really, what are you doing here?"

"I was hoping you'd let me take a look at the cannon."

Her eyebrow rose. "You came all the way out to my ship to ask for a favor?"

"No." Jackson stalked forward, closing the gap between them. His forearms bumped against the solid wooden door, coming to rest on either side of her head. "I came here because I couldn't stop thinking about doing this."

Heat flared deep inside her steady gaze. She didn't blink or try to cover it up. She let him see exactly what she wanted—him.

Good thing that was what he wanted, too.

Bringing their mouths together, he let his lips brush softly against hers. Over and over again, he teased them both until she was panting, chasing his mouth for more each time he pulled out of her reach.

Her fingers curled into his biceps, held tight and tried to compel him closer.

Never in his life had he wanted a woman so much, and from nothing more than a few kisses. He was so hard he ached. But the funny thing was the ache wasn't just below his belt. His entire body throbbed with the desire to touch and taste and *know* her, inside and out.

This woman drove him crazy. He shouldn't want anything to do with her. He couldn't trust her. But none of that mattered. She'd gotten inside his head and wasn't letting go.

"Aw, hell," he breathed, unable to keep up the torture anymore. Burying his hand at her nape, Jackson angled her head so that he could kiss her hard.

Their tongues tangled. She sucked his bottom lip into her mouth, scraped her teeth along the sensitive edge and made his cock leap as if she'd run her teeth over it instead.

They were both panting when a loud siren split the air.

LORALEI JERKED BACKWARD. Her lungs stuttered inside her chest. Sirens were never good. She wasn't very familiar with life on a ship, but she knew that much.

The familiar band constricted, threatening to cut off her air supply. Every muscle in her body froze and her mind began to spin on the worst-case scenario. They were going down.

Everyone was going to die. She was going to die.

This was why she hadn't wanted to come on a ship in the middle of the open sea in the first place.

As if sensing her rising panic, Jackson wrapped his hands around her jaw and forced her to face him. He brought them close, until all she could see was the calm, steady blue of his gaze.

"Take a deep breath, Loralei."

As always, her body obeyed him. Her lungs expanded, drawing deeply until her chest filled.

"That's it," he said, gifting her with a soft, approving smile that suddenly had all the tension leaking out of her body.

"Let's go see what's happening."

Grasping her hand, Jackson led her into the hallway where they encountered a couple of her crew. She didn't miss the way their gazes snagged on her hand in Jackson's.

She snatched it away and tucked it tight against her body, but continued to follow behind him.

Together, the knot of people pushed onto the upper deck to utter chaos.

Brian was shouting. The captain was directing several of the crew who were running across the deck.

Before she could ask, Jackson stalked up to Brian and said, "What the hell is going on?"

Brian glared at him and then deliberately turned away without answering.

She didn't need to know Jackson well to understand that wouldn't go over well.

Grasping the other man by the arm, Jackson spun him. "I asked you a question. What the hell is going on?"

From nearby one of the crew answered. "We're taking on water. Not sure how or why, but it isn't good."

The panic that had receded before leapt back in full force.

"Have you tried to locate the leak?"

Brian frowned. "Of course. We sent a diver down, but he couldn't find the source. We've sealed the bulkhead to contain it, but it won't be long before she starts listing."

Jackson swore and dropped Brian's arm. "Everyone get to the launches. The *Amphitrite* is close. Head there."

Turning to her, Jackson ran his hands down her arms in a soothing gesture she needed too much to pull away from. "Get whatever you need, Loralei. We have some time, but hurry."

Then he was striding off across the deck toward the captain.

She watched him go, unable to look away. He wore the mantle of authority with such ease. He'd taken over her crew and ship without a second thought. He knew exactly how to handle the situation.

Without him she'd have been frozen in place.

Although that didn't mean it sat well with her. In fact, she didn't like depending on him. Or anyone, really.

She was used to being alone and letting him take command felt like giving him more control over not just her crew and ship but her mind and will, as well.

She had to regain some authority.

Stepping forward, she insinuated herself back into the conversation between Jackson and her captain.

"I don't care what you say, I'm going down there to see if I can find the leak. I don't have much faith in your divers or their ability to find their ass with both hands."

Loralei gasped and then growled low in her throat. It was maddening, and enlightening, to hear Jackson's opinion of her crew. Although, it shouldn't have come as a surprise. It wasn't like he hadn't alluded to it several times.

But it was one thing to read between the lines and another to hear him spell it out.

"This is my ship, Jackson."

He turned to include her in the conversation, a scowl marring his face. "I know that."

"No, apparently you don't. I didn't ask you to take over and direct my crew."

He turned fully to face her, crossing his arms over his chest. "No, you didn't. But that's not going to stop me from doing what I need to."

"My crew's already been down there." And the thought of Jackson diving right now, with the ship taking on water had her chest aching again.

If the *Emily* was going to start listing, it could be dangerous for anyone in the water. "No."

"What?"

"No, you're not going down there."

Crossing his arms over his chest, Jackson spread his feet wide on the deck and glared at her. "And just how do you expect to stop me?"

"Easy." Turning, she yelled to Brian. "No one give him any dive equipment."

From across the deck, Brian grinned. "You got it, boss."

Jackson made a low, frustrated sound. Tough.

She felt him behind her, pressing in close to her back. The heat of him. His anger.

She expected him to lash out or get upset, but he did neither. Instead, he leaned in and murmured against her ear, "You'd better get whatever you want to take with you because I'm putting your ass in a boat in five minutes whether you're ready or not."

Loralei spun to argue, but the minute her gaze collided with his she realized he wasn't kidding. And he had the strength to back up the threat.

Gritting her teeth, Loralei raced back below deck. She grabbed up her laptop, her research and the files of information she'd gathered on the *Chimera* over the past few weeks.

Snatching a random handful of clothes, she stuffed everything into a bag and headed back up. By the time she got there most everyone else had gathered by the boats.

When Brian had given her the standard safety briefing she'd never actually expected to use the information. Someone had pulled out the life vests, although most of the crew hadn't bothered to put them on.

Jackson wrapped an arm around her waist and propelled her into the launch. Without bothering to ask, he grabbed the bags from her shoulders and tucked them beneath her seat.

They were several feet away from the *Emily* before a thought burst through Loralei's mind. Standing up, she frantically started counting heads.

The boat rocked beneath her feet, but she was too preoccupied with making sure everyone she was responsible for had gotten off the ship.

Jackson's hand wrapped around her hip, trying to pull her back into her seat.

"What the hell are you doing, Loralei? Sit down."

She resisted him. "Counting my people."

The fingers digging into her side gentled.

"Everyone's fine and accounted for."

The total in her head matched the number of her crew. The frantic pace of her heartbeat slowed. Dropping back onto the seat, Loralei buried her head in her hands.

Her entire body was shaking, with adrenaline and fear. Jackson's arm slipped around her, his hand smoothing up and down her back.

"Hey. It's okay."

Mumbling between her fingers, she said, "I should have handled that better. Should have been more prepared."

"You did fine."

She rolled her head sideways, looking at him through the gaps between her fingers. "I froze. All I could think about was plunging into the water and sinking under the surface, of someone else getting hurt, trapped and dead," she whispered, careful to keep the words just between the two of them.

"Understandable."

Jackson's calm, even tone grated on her nerves. Her insides were a jumbled mess. Her brain, her guts and everything in between felt scrambled.

He was so damn pragmatic. Accepting.

"How do you do it? How do you stay so damn calm?"

"Years and years of practice. I've been in a hell of a lot worse situations, Loralei. That was nothing. Everyone on your crew did exactly what they were trained to do."

Dropping her hands, Loralei looked back at the *Emily*. The ship was listing slightly to one side, but appeared to be holding her own. Sealing off the bulkhead meant the flooding would be contained. While the ship was damaged, and would be impossible to sail, at least she shouldn't sink.

"The cannon." She sighed.

"Will be fine. We'll call in for a tugboat to come and pick her up and haul her back to port. You can rent a replacement ship from the marina to arrive with the tug."

They reached the *Amphitrite*, pulling alongside her. Jackson's crew gathered on the deck, no doubt curious as to what was going on.

One by one, everyone climbed out. Jackson kept his arm wrapped around her shoulders, tucking her close against his body.

Part of her knew she should push him away, but she couldn't find the strength to actually do it.

Not even when she looked across the knot of humanity milling about to find Brian glaring holes into Jackson.

11

JACKSON SHUFFLED EVERYONE. His crew wasn't thrilled, but they were out in the open ocean and none of them would have been okay with leaving the Lancaster team adrift on a disabled, listing ship.

He left Marcus to assign berths while he showed Loralei to his cabin.

The minute he ushered her inside and shut the door behind them he knew he'd made a mistake.

She spun on her heel and he could clearly read the irritation and anger that tightened her features.

"A little presumptuous, aren't you? Just because we had sex last night doesn't mean I'm going to bunk with you."

Jackson's lips twitched. Loralei's gaze zeroed in on the gesture and her light green eyes flashed with a hidden fire that immediately sparked something deep in his blood.

Pulling out a drawer, he didn't bother looking inside before grabbing some clothes.

"I was planning on bunking with Marcus."

Her eyes widened and she shifted uncomfortably on her feet. "Oh."

There was something satisfying about knowing he

could set her off-kilter. That he could affect her just as much as she affected him.

Crossing to her, Jackson crowded into her personal space. He liked that she didn't back away from him. Instead, she tipped her head back and stood her ground, staring at him.

With his hands still gripping the clothes, he bracketed her hips and pulled her tight against his body, nestling his half-hard erection against her heat.

She sucked in a harsh breath. Her pupils dilated and her body went lax.

"I wouldn't do that to you, Loralei. As much as I'd love to stay here and share this bed with you tonight, I worry about what your crew might think."

He was trying to do the right thing, but Loralei wasn't making it easy. Her lush, pink lips were parted in an open invitation he couldn't seem to ignore.

Bending down, he captured her mouth. Sweeping inside, he drank in her sweet taste. The kiss had an edge of desperation. Evidence of the banked hunger they were both fighting.

Finally, he found the strength to pull away, and left before he lost the will to do so.

What was it about her that drove him insane but also brought out his protective instincts?

He wasn't used to worrying about any woman aside from his sister and stepmother. None of the women he'd dated over the years had called up this kind of concern.

But then he supposed he hadn't let himself get close to them. He wasn't interested in taking that risk. In opening himself up to someone only to have them rip out his heart, as his mom had done to his dad.

His first instinct when those alarms had started going off, though, was to protect Loralei.

He'd seen the panic wash over her. He'd wanted to fix it. To do whatever he could to make the fear in her eyes disappear.

His brain told him not to trust Loralei, but his body didn't seem to give a damn. His instincts, either.

So bunking with Marcus was a smart idea—for both of them.

HOURS LATER, LORALEI was restless. The sun had set shortly after they'd come aboard the *Amphitrite*. Jackson's crew had prepared a dinner everyone shared. The evening had been filled with awkwardness, and not just between her and Jackson.

Everyone on board was being careful about what they said and how they said it. Her crew kept to one side of the dining room while the Trident crew occupied the other.

She'd tried not to notice the way Jackson interacted with his team. He was clearly in charge, but still managed to be one of the guys. They joked and shared a comfortable camaraderie that she hadn't realized her team was missing until she'd seen it in his.

Oh, the Lancaster team worked together well enough. And in the evenings they managed to stay busy and entertained. They'd worked together for years, had shared experiences. But something was missing.

Maybe it was Jackson's years working in the SEAL Teams that allowed him to foster that kind of atmosphere among the guys. His crew had certainly been together less time than hers.

Now it was late. The ship was quiet. And she couldn't sleep. Lying in Jackson's bed had left her fidgety and achy in a way she didn't want to explore. Needing a distraction, Loralei threw on some shorts and a tank and headed out into the quiet ship.

Dim, florescent lights illuminated the corridor. She could head up to the top deck, but after the events of the day she didn't think testing the boundaries of her fear in the dark was a smart idea.

Instead, she turned in the other direction. Most of the doors she passed were closed, but the one leading to the office she'd seen the first night she'd snuck onto the *Amphitrite* stood open.

Maybe she'd find Jackson there.

She shouldn't be looking for him. The restlessness throbbing through her body told her searching him out was a very bad idea. Yet, that didn't stop her from drawing closer.

It quickly became obvious he wasn't there. The room was dark, just as she'd found it the first night. Although tonight a laptop that hadn't been there before sat open on the table.

It was on, faint light spilling from the screen.

Drawn to it, Loralei found herself staring down at the information highlighted there. Several screens were open, tiled one over the other in a way that beckoned her to look.

Information. Documents. Charts.

The historian in her couldn't stop reading the details, drinking in the data. Her instinct was to record it.

Grabbing out her phone, Loralei leaned close and snapped picture after picture of each open window.

The minute she clicked through the last screen Loralei's belly began to churn with regret and guilt. But not enough to delete the pictures.

It wasn't as if she'd be able to unsee what she'd read, anyway.

She knew the information on those screens. It was eerily similar to what she'd found in her father's office.

Although, there were a few differences. The question became had her father uncovered it first or had Jackson.

Right now, she didn't know the answer and didn't have time to dwell on it.

It was possible Jackson had discovered something she hadn't. For the past few days she'd been fighting the feeling she was missing something. Something very important.

That she just wasn't seeing a piece of the puzzle.

It wasn't the first time she'd encountered the sensation, and it always drove her crazy when she did. She hated to be out of the loop or left in the dark. Maybe that was what made her a good historian.

Pushing away from the table, Loralei returned to the hallway.

She headed for the galley. Maybe a midnight snack would help settle her. If nothing else, it would give her hands something to do as her mind worked through how she was going to handle this.

Flipping on the lights, she surveyed the empty room. It was stark and industrial, everything put away in its place… for now. She was about to make a mess.

It was one of the things she loved about cooking, something she often did when she was upset or unsettled. It was a trick her grandmother had taught her, to channel the energy into something productive.

She really wanted to make something chocolaty and gooey, like walnut and caramel brownies. However, the pantry had definitely been stocked by men. The abundance of staples such as canned food, peanut butter and dried beef products had her scrunching her nose with distaste.

Luckily, she did manage to find a couple packages of chocolate chips, a container of oatmeal, some raisins, flour, sugar, butter and vanilla. They weren't going to be anything spectacular, but at least she could make some cookies.

With everything spread across the stainless steel table that doubled as counter space, and the oven set to preheat, Loralei started mixing ingredients.

She didn't bother measuring anything, just dumped and adjusted as necessary. After a few minutes, that itchy, uncomfortable feeling that had lodged in the center of her spine eased. She hummed, twisting her body to a melody only she could hear in her head, wishing like hell she'd thought to grab her earbuds so she could listen to some music.

She plopped dough on to a greased cookie sheet. Wiggling her rear, she bent down to put the first batch into the oven before shutting the door with a pop of her hip.

Spinning around, she was headed back to the table for another round when movement caught her eye.

She gasped, her heart kicking against her ribs.

Jackson stood in the doorway, arms crossed over his massive chest. His body was completely relaxed, leaning against the jamb in a way that told her without asking that he'd been there awhile.

"Jesus, you scared the crap out of me," she said, scowling. She picked up another pan and set it on the counter. Reaching for the stick of butter, she grasped the end and ran it lightly along the surface.

"We have that spray stuff."

Loralei wrinkled her nose. "Do you know how many preservatives and artificial ingredients are in that? You might as well spray chemicals directly onto your cookies."

"Because chemicals are worse than sugar at—" he rolled his wrist to look at the face of his complicated watch "—half-past midnight."

She shrugged. He had a point, but she wasn't ready to concede it.

"What are you doing, Loralei?"

She shot him an incredulous look, but answered anyway. "Baking cookies."

"Okay, but why? And why now?"

She reached for the bowl of chocolate-chip cookie dough and began spooning another batch onto the greased sheet. "I couldn't sleep. This is what I do when I'm restless."

"You bake?"

"Don't sound so surprised."

Jackson moved farther into the room. For the first time since she'd walked in, the space felt small. He stopped on the other side of the table, but that didn't help much.

His hands pressed flat against the shiny, silvery surface. She couldn't stop staring at them. They were strong and tanned, with a sprinkling of blond hair.

She could remember them running up and down her body. The way he'd touched and teased, awakening nerve endings and desires she hadn't felt in a very long time.

Loralei swallowed and dragged her gaze back to the bowl.

"I'm not."

"My grandmother and I would make cookies together whenever either of us was upset. Or when I had a bad day at school. When some boy broke my heart. We'd bake. Mostly in silence, just the familiar comfort and routine."

Loralei smiled at the memories. They were some of her favorites. Behind her, the timer she'd set began to buzz. Twisting away, she pulled the hot pan from the oven and popped in the second one.

After setting it on the table, she reached for a spatula to

transfer the cookies to the rack she'd found tucked away with the cookie sheets.

Jackson didn't bother to wait. He snatched one straight from the pan, tossing it back and forth between his hands so that it wouldn't burn his fingers. He broke it in half and somehow managed to blow on the cookie at the same time he shoved it into his mouth. He chewed and swallowed.

For some reason Loralei's shoulders tightened as she waited to hear his verdict.

Everything loosened again when he let out a groan of delight, his eyes slipping shut in ecstasy.

"I'm sure it didn't hurt that when you were done there were always warm, gooey treats to share. These are so damn good. A hell of a lot better than anything from a package."

She tossed him a saucy grin. "That's what happens when you use real ingredients instead of the crap in a can or box."

His cocky grin, the one that both set her on edge and managed to leave her feeling effervescent inside, slowly melted away. With deliberate movements, Jackson rounded the table. It wasn't quick. She had plenty of time to shift.

But she didn't. She couldn't. If she was honest, this was exactly what she'd been looking for when she left her room. And would have been so much easier to deal with if she hadn't made her little detour first.

She expected him to crowd into her personal space, to kiss her and take the choice out of her hands. It would have been less complicated if he'd done that.

Instead he reached for her hair, pinched a lock between his forefinger and thumb and ran down it. Her scalp tingled.

He continued to rake her with that intense stare, but there was something else beneath it, not just hunger, but real concern. "What's wrong?"

"Nothing."

"You're a terrible liar."

Loralei sighed. She moved away from him, reaching for the ingredients to mix together her oatmeal raisin cookies.

But Jackson wasn't willing to let her get away with that distraction anymore. He shifted right along with her, sliding down the counter as she moved and stirred.

"You're worried."

"Yeah, I'm worried." Anyone in her situation would be worried. "My ship is in danger of sinking."

"It isn't. Your team sealed the bulkhead and contained the leak before we left the *Emily*."

"Great," she said, tossing her hands and sending a small puff of flour into the air. "That's perfect, because either way I'm going to have to pay for a tow back to the marina and hire a new ship to finish this trip, spending money I don't actually have going after a treasure I might never find."

Loralei heard the desperation in her voice and hated herself just a little bit for it. Even more for revealing it to Jackson. It shouldn't matter this much. But it did.

Tears burned her eyelids. She kept her gaze trained on the dough, taking out her frustrations and emotions on the hapless pile of ingredients.

She'd wanted to find the *Chimera* for her father. For herself. And up until this afternoon, she'd thought maybe, just maybe, she could pull it off. Share this one thing with the father she'd never really had a chance to know. But now...

"We're dead in the water and there's no way we're going to beat your crew to the *Chimera*."

HE WANTED TO comfort her. He shouldn't want to, but he did.

"We're not going to leave you here alone with a disabled ship."

He should feel frustrated. The *Emily*'s troubles were going to delay his own search for the *Chimera*.

But even if he could get his team and equipment to the next dive site, he wasn't willing to leave Loralei and her team alone to ramble around the *Amphitrite* unchecked.

That was just asking for trouble.

Taking a break from the paperwork and research he'd been doing to keep his mind off the woman occupying his bed, Jackson had taken a stroll up to the top deck. On his way back he'd been surprised to see the light on in the galley. Even more so that Loralei had been the one inside. He'd thought her asleep a long time ago.

He'd hung back for a bit, wondering just what she'd been up to. Baking cookies hadn't been on his list of possibilities.

Stepping closer now, Jackson purposely moved into her space. She didn't look at him, but she didn't have to for him to gauge her reaction.

He'd been trained to notice miniscule details. The way her grip on the mixing spoon tightened. Or how her body instinctively dipped toward him. Her parted lips and increased pulse.

She was aware of him, even if she didn't want to be.

Using a single finger, he slipped it beneath the thin strap of the tank top she was wearing. Her skin was so soft and smooth. It invited him to touch more.

Last night had been an explosion of pent-up lust. Right now, he wanted to spread her across the stainless steel and make a feast out of her.

Her body began to quiver beneath his gentle caress. He could feel the tremors she was desperately trying to deny.

"Don't," she whispered.

He should listen to her, and not just because he'd always been the kind of man who took no as an absolute response. Loralei Lancaster was going to be the death of him.

But at least he'd die with a smile on his face.

Burying his nose in the cloud of her hair, he breathed deep, pulled her scent into his lungs. Tonight that signature sweet fragrance he'd come to associate with her was combined with the tang of semisweet chocolate.

There was something about a woman who baked that always got to him. Maybe it was because his mom hadn't been much of a cook. Or because his stepmom had been, bringing that taste of domestic normalcy into his life when he'd needed it most.

Either way, he should have known to turn around and walk away the moment Loralei had started pulling out ingredients.

It was way too late for that now.

"Do you really mean that?" he asked, running his lips up the side of her neck, not quite kissing her, but not letting her go, either.

Loralei melted against him. It was an undeniable sign that her body was lost to the same cravings overwhelming him. But he needed the words. Gripping her hips, Jackson turned her, pressing her back against the counter.

"Do you want me to stop, Loralei?" he asked, staring down at her.

Jackson watched the rise and fall of her chest as she drew in several shallow breaths. Her struggle fascinated him, probably more than it should have. Maybe because he was fighting the same things. Would what she wanted outweigh what she thought she should do?

It obviously had for him—more than once.

"No," she finally breathed out, desire winning over reason.

Without another word, Jackson turned away.

She reached for him, grabbing onto his arm.

Anger chased across her face. "You bastard. You just wanted to hear me admit that I wanted you, didn't you?"

Jackson shot a glance over his shoulder, letting the heat of his desire singe her. He didn't bother answering, instead flipping the knob on the oven.

Her eyes followed his every movement, eating each deliberate step with interest.

Turning back, he swept her into his arms.

"We've had enough disaster for one day, don't you think?"

12

JACKSON WASN'T WRONG. Loralei had had more than enough disaster to last a lifetime.

Cradled tight against his body, she couldn't think of a better place to be to soothe her jagged nerves. She'd been trying to avoid this from the moment she'd stepped onto the *Amphitrite*, but it was absolutely inevitable.

She couldn't be this close to Jackson and not want him. The need went deep. It was an addiction, that thing her brain told her she shouldn't have, but her body craved.

Her body was winning tonight.

Palming her thighs, Jackson wrapped them around his waist and strode out of the galley. In that moment, she didn't care where he was taking her, as long as it meant they'd both get what they wanted.

Loralei wrapped her arms around his neck, pressing closer, but a sudden thought stopped her.

"What if someone sees us?"

Jackson paused in the hallway, sending a spike of anxiety through Loralei.

"No, don't stop." Why was he standing still? She wanted him to keep going. Loralei squirmed, but Jackson simply tightened his hold on her.

"I don't care, princess. It's no one's business what's going on between us."

"Yeah, right," she scoffed. That's what he thought.

She had no idea what his crew would think if one of them wandered into the hallway and saw Jackson holding her this way. But she had a damn good idea what her team would think. Brian would be the ringleader in an attempt to pound the shit out of Jackson.

And that was a mess she didn't have the energy to deal with tonight.

Brian had clearly been spoiling for a fight from the moment Jackson had boarded *Emily's Fortune*. There was definitely tension between them, and she sensed there was more to it than Trident stealing Lancaster's clients.

But that was a thought for another time.

Jackson probably would get a pat on the back from his guys for landing the only female on the ship. She definitely had the most to lose here if they were discovered.

But there was more than one way to compel him into action.

Using her clasped hands behind his neck, Loralei used her thighs and levered herself up until she could reach his mouth. She kissed him, diving straight into the sensation of his lips against hers.

They fought for control of the kiss, tongues tangling in a thrust and retreat that left her panting. Pulling back, she scraped her teeth across his bottom lip and growled, "Get a move on, ace."

And he did exactly as she commanded, his purposeful strides eating ground at lightning speed until the cabin door was shut firmly behind them. The rest of the world— the rest of the ship—was blocked out.

Slowly, Jackson let her body slide down his, igniting all sorts of nerve endings.

Her feet hit the floor and she swayed. The only thing keeping her upright were his hands on her. But before she could regain her balance, Jackson spun her around. The room revolved, everything blurring away except for the heat emanating off his skin, the familiar scent of him.

Pressing her back to his front, Jackson let his fingers slip beneath the hem of her shirt and dragged it up her stomach in a cotton-covered caress.

There was no point in fighting—herself or him. Loralei let her head drop back to his shoulder, relishing the way his strong body caught hers. The only time they separated was when he lifted her shirt over her head.

Those moments apart felt like agony. Loralei counted them with her pulse and the soft puffs of Jackson's ragged breaths.

This was what she'd been trying not to think about all day. The feel of him. The way he made her mindless and needy and…so completely focused that she didn't give a damn about the treasure. Or worry about the pressure of finding it and saving her father's legacy. Or the job she'd left behind in Chicago, part of her stable life that was starting to feel more like a prison the longer she spent beneath the tropical sun.

Not when Jackson was touching her.

When his skin blazed against hers that was all that mattered. All that existed in her universe.

The unforgiving pressure of his mouth latched onto her neck. Her shoulder. Sucking, teasing, biting. Prickles chased across her skin and she could feel his satisfaction with her response in the cocky curve of his lips.

She wanted to make him pay for his arrogance, but couldn't keep her thoughts from fracturing enough to do it. Not when his fingers were running teasing circles around her navel and across the skin at the waistband of her shorts.

Later. She'd make him beg, later.

"God, I love the way you respond to me," he whispered into her skin. "Do you know how gorgeous you look with your skin flushed and your deep green eyes unfocused?"

Okay, maybe not.

"I love knowing I can do that to you. Make you forget everything but the pleasure I can give you."

She loved that, too. More than she should, but she'd worry about that later.

At some point Jackson had slipped open her fly, she had no idea when. But she noticed when he plunged his fingers deep into her panties, finding the slick core of her sex.

Loralei gasped, arched her hips forward. An unintelligible sound ripped through her chest, reverence and pleading mixed together.

His other hand found the clasp of her bra between her shoulder blades and snapped it open. She hadn't dressed for him—or anyone—today. Her underwear wasn't silk and lace, but plain cotton. It had never bothered her before, but right now she wished she was dressed like a siren instead of the staid historian she actually was.

Not that Jackson seemed to give a damn.

He let her bra fall to the floor at her feet and then immediately pushed her shorts and panties off her hips.

She was perfectly naked, and once again he was fully clothed.

Loralei tried to turn in his arms so she could return the favor. But his roughened hands tightened on her hips, holding her in place.

His arm snaked around her waist, crushing her to him. Her spine arched until her butt pressed firmly against his growing erection.

Loralei tipped her head back, trying to look at him and figure out what he was doing. What he wanted.

And it was clear as soon as she caught his gaze. Half a foot taller than she was, from his vantage point, Jackson had the perfect view of her body. And from the animalistic heat blazing from his eyes, he was relishing it.

His gaze devoured every inch of her.

Loralei had never felt so exposed—so desired—in her life. Her skin actually pulsed with it.

She pulled in a rough gasp, appreciating the way his eyes went dark and a bit dangerous as her chest rose and fell with the stuttered breath.

"God, Loralei." His voice was midnight heat, smooth and low. And if he didn't touch her soon, she was going to spontaneously combust.

As if sensing just how close to the edge he'd pushed her, Jackson chose that moment to give her what she needed.

Starting at her collarbone, he traced the delicate curves of her body with a single fingertip. The caress was light. Torture. Especially combined with the sharp cut of his possessive stare.

Why did it feel as if he was claiming every inch he touched? For his use. Her pleasure.

What should have bothered her was how much she wanted him to take every inch of her. But it didn't. How could it when she knew exactly how expertly he could handle her? How much she could trust him. At least with her body.

His hand slipped over her tummy, making her muscles jump and leaving a restless, tickling sensation that spread out from her center. Anticipation. That's what it was.

She had no idea what he was going to do next. And that excited her. Left her breathless.

Slowly, his fingers curled over her sex. He teased the crease at her hip, brushed across her clit. Heat spread, turning her insides liquid.

She had no idea how long he stayed there, gently pulling at the close-cropped curls covering her. Caressing her. Driving her crazy. Long enough that she was so slick with need she could feel the moist heat of her own desire coating her skin. His fingers.

The urge to squirm was a building thing, deep inside, but his other arm held her tight against the solid wall of his body.

Please, please, please was the litany running over and over inside her head. It was possible she said the words aloud, but she wasn't entirely certain.

But there was no mistaking the cry of relief that erupted from her lips when he finally spread her sex wide and dipped inside. She was so close that she was afraid the first real touch would send her immediately over the edge.

Not what she wanted. She needed to feel him, hot and thick inside her.

Loralei tried to pull away, but instead of letting her go, Jackson curved his other hand around the edge of her jaw. With gentle pressure, he directed her gaze across the room to the mirror bolted to the wall. She'd forgotten it was there.

The sight reflected there nearly made her knees collapse.

There was a wanton woman practically draped across Jackson's tall, delicious body.

There was something wholly erotic about the image. Not just the vision of her own naked body, but the sharp pull of Jackson's features. The way his eyes consumed her, in the mirror, outside the reflection. He kept looking back and forth between the two as if he couldn't decide which view was better.

Greedy man, he wanted them both. But then so did she. Raising her arms, Loralei slowly clasped her fingers behind his neck, arching her body and stretching up on tiptoe. She'd never been one to stare at herself. She wasn't the vain type.

But tonight she could admit she was amazing. Because he made her feel amazing.

The low growl that slipped through his lips and rumbled across her skin made her bold.

As his right hand played with her sex, teasing the entrance to her body, brushing terrifyingly softly across her clit, his left dropped to her breast and pinched an already aching nipple between thumb and forefinger.

Neither one of them could pull their gaze away. Together, they finally watched his fingers disappear inside her body. Loralei whimpered, her eyelids threatening to close on the sweet pleasure.

"Watch," Jackson ground out, somehow managing to make the demand gentle. Maybe it was the slight tremor to the single word. The realization that though she hadn't touched him yet, he was as close to the edge as she was.

She could feel the hard press of his erection caught between them. It was maddening knowing how much he wanted her, but being unable to do anything about it.

In and out, again and again, together they watched him work over her body. Somehow watching him in the mirror amplified the slide of each plunge, the emptiness of each retreat.

Loralei could feel the orgasm building inside her, powerful and overwhelming. She knew the explosion was coming, but could do nothing to stop the swell and pressure.

And then it was there, dragging a cry from her parted lips. She trembled with the force of it, grateful for Jackson's arm around her to hold her steady. He murmured words, the cadence of them registering even if the actual meaning didn't.

Her brain clicked back into gear and she blinked to find them still facing the mirror, but at some point Jackson had managed to shed his clothes.

He was still behind her. Holding her. The heat of him practically burning into her.

His cock thrust between them, pressed hard and heavy against the small of her back. Loralei's hips made an involuntary movement, a pulse and slide that had him sucking in a hard breath.

How could she want him—no, need him—after that mind-blowing orgasm?

But there was no denying her body's reaction.

She knew it. Jackson saw it. And that damn wicked smirk was back on his lips. But before she could do anything about it, the flat of his palm was pressing between her shoulder blades.

It was instinctive, the way she folded beneath the pressure, her own palms flattening against the low surface of the mattress in front of her. Tapping her feet, Jackson silently asked her to spread wide for him.

Leaning forward, he murmured in her ear, "Don't take your eyes off the mirror."

As if she could have pulled her gaze away from him if she'd wanted to. Jackson Duchane was a force to be reckoned with fully clothed. His body was a work of art, muscles, bones and tendons coming together in a form that was as close to perfect as humanly possible.

She wanted to run her hands over every inch of him, explore the bulges and indents. The strength and tension and sinew that made him the man he was.

Loralei watched him position himself behind her. Unable to help herself, she licked her lips and then dragged the bottom one between her teeth. Jackson's gaze snagged there for several moments. His nostrils flared on a heavy breath, as if he was fighting for control.

The first time had been unintentional. But with a wicked thrill coursing through her, Loralei repeated the movement, this time giving her hips a wiggle so that she grazed against the throbbing length of his erection.

His eyes went wild. That was the only way she could describe his reaction. She practically watched the thread to the restraint he'd been clinging to snap.

Jackson grasped her hips, his fingers digging into her as he held her steady.

He stood above her, bronzed skin gleaming with the sheen of sweat, every muscle bunched hard and tight.

She felt him at her entrance, the wide head of his erection pressing against the opening of her body.

But better than that, she watched as he disappeared inside, inch by delicious inch. Stretching her. Loralei let out a tiny whimper when his hips pressed against her as he seated himself all the way deep inside. He stayed there for several seconds, letting her body adjust.

Her arms trembled, not from holding herself up, but from the electrical storm shooting through her nervous system.

And then he was moving in and out, claiming her body. Loralei watched as his sex slid out of her, wet and gleaming with her own desire, before disappearing again. He was slow and deliberate at first. She wasn't even aware of moving her own hips, but suddenly she noticed she wasn't just keeping up with his rhythm, but begging Jackson to go faster and harder.

They were both panting. Her fingers curled into the sheets, popping the corners off as the tension wound tighter inside her. The first orgasm had been mind-numbing. The second was right there, rippling on the edge of her consciousness. And she wanted it. So bad. But she wanted to feel him let go more.

For the first time since he bent her forward, Loralei tore her gaze away from the reflection where their bodies joined and instead found Jackson's gaze. And realized he'd been watching her the whole time. Not the sway of her breasts with each of his pounding thrusts or the way he claimed her body. But her face. Her eyes and mouth.

And the moment she saw that, Loralei felt the first flutters of the orgasm slam into her. "Oh, holy…"

Jackson groaned, his eyes sliding closed and his thrusts going completely erratic. He buried himself deep inside her, fingers gripping hard to her hips. Just before she surrendered to the orgasm, she felt the kick of his release. The muscles of her sex clamped tight, holding him deep inside her body, just before the breath-stealing contractions of her own release pulled her down into oblivion.

Together, they collapsed onto the bed. Or maybe she collapsed, her legs and arms refusing to hold her up any longer. Somehow, Jackson managed to roll them so they lay diagonally across the bed.

He was still buried deep inside her. Loralei knew she should let him get up, go back to his temporary bed in Marcus's quarters. But several minutes later, when he stirred as if to do that, she clamped her hands on the arms he'd banded around her body and held on tight.

"No, don't go. Not yet."

What they'd just shared had been down and dirty. And, yet, Loralei had never felt so connected with anyone in her life. Maybe it was because she'd shown him the vulnerability beneath the perfect facade. Or maybe she was a victim of her own hormones. She had no clue.

But either way, she wasn't ready for him to leave. Not yet.

13

SHE'D ASKED HIM to stay. And he wanted to. It wasn't that he'd never spent the night with a woman. He had. It was more like he'd never really thought about it one way or the other.

Before, sleep had simply been something that followed sex. He'd never been the kind to cuddle or spoon. Once the sex was over, he didn't have a compulsive urge to touch his lover.

Until Loralei.

Eventually, he did get up, pad to the attached bathroom and clean up a bit. But the entire time, he'd wanted to be back in that bed with her. In his bed. Actually, he'd wanted to be buried inside her body. Not necessarily for the orgasm that would follow, but for the sensation of being connected to her in the most physical way possible.

That should have had him making some excuse to hightail it away from her. Instead, he found himself crawling back into the bed beside her. He didn't wait for her to roll to him, but snagged her around the waist and settled her soft curves against his body, an arm and leg slung possessively over her.

Holding her felt right, but his brain told him this wasn't

a good idea. That sooner or later he'd regret letting his guard down around her—and he was betting on sooner.

Yet he couldn't make himself pull away again. At least not right now when his body was still languid and his brain was sated.

Jackson closed his eyes and willed the voice in his head that kept whispering she was using him and would drop him at the first sign that he wasn't useful anymore, to go the hell away.

Loralei spoke. Up until that point he'd thought she was half asleep. Her body had been relaxed and boneless, her breathing deep and rhythmic.

But there was no hint of drowsiness in her words.

"We identified the cannon as the *Chimera*'s."

Jackson stiffened. Why was she telling him this? And right now. He wanted to take her offer of information at face value, but his training made him immediately look for an ulterior motive.

"You don't have to tell me that."

She glanced over her shoulder, searching his face for several seconds before her eyes crinkled at the corners. "I know." Her hand, where it rested on his wrist, tightened. And for some reason that was enough to make the tension melt from his body.

Turning her head, she burrowed deeper into the pillows, into the curve of his body around hers.

"I felt this…thrill when Eric told me it was definitely from the *Chimera*."

He'd bet. For a moment, Jackson had to beat back the tiny curl of jealousy that slipped through his belly. He didn't want to have the reaction, but it was hard to fight it down.

Loralei's team had something he'd worked years to get. And it had more or less fallen into their laps. All his life his father and stepmother had drilled into him that hard work was rewarded. The Teams had reinforced that idea, allowing only the strongest to enter their ranks.

He wasn't a child, throwing a tantrum because the world wasn't fair. He'd seen enough death and destruction to know there wasn't always reason behind actions or events.

But that didn't stop him from thinking the world *should* work that way. Or being bothered when it didn't.

Especially when the injustice was personal. Loralei might not have stolen the information, but he'd told her it was stolen and she'd still gone ahead and used it.

Didn't that make her just as guilty? A few days ago the answer to that question had been black and white. Tonight, it was colored in shades of gray.

But that was an issue for another time and another place. Outside the bed they'd just shared together. For tonight, he was going to put all that aside and just listen to what she was telling him.

Or, at least, he was going to try.

Unaware of his internal struggle, Loralei kept talking.

"I… It was unexpected."

"That the cannon was theirs?" Because his gut had told him it was as soon as Loralei's team had raised the artifact. Those instincts had saved his life—Asher's and Knox's, as well—on more than one occasion.

"No, that it mattered to me. That I could get a little lightheaded with the thrill of that discovery. Although, it shouldn't have."

She said the last sentence with a tinge of bitterness that he didn't quite understand.

"Why not?"

Her entire body lifted and held as she drew in a deep

breath and then let it out on a noisy sigh. "I spend my days with books and documents and students."

That was something he already knew. She had a PhD and worked as a professor and researcher, or had until her father's death and subsequent bequeathal of Lancaster Diving and Salvage.

But instead of telling her he'd checked into her before arriving on Turks and Caicos, he kept his mouth shut. Something told him the minute he admitted the truth her words would dry up.

And he really wanted to know where she was going with this.

"I spend my time trying to pass on a love of history to young men and women who couldn't care less. They see my class as an obstacle they have to overcome in order to make it wherever they truly want to go. It pisses me off." The words came out like a confession, pulled from her so reluctantly that they were low and soft.

"I don't understand."

"Everyone today is in such a hurry—to get somewhere, to do something. Focused so intently on the future that they forget to pay attention to the past. To the lessons our ancestors learned and hoped to pass down to us so that we could do better."

She wasn't telling him anything he didn't already know. "I've been to war, Loralei," he murmured. "I understand."

Her fingers tightened around his wrist for a moment before releasing. She stroked her hand down his arm, the caress raising the tiny hairs as it passed.

"I suppose you do, but not everyone does. And I realized yesterday that I don't really, either. I've been stuck between those dusty shelves, riding my high horse, absolutely refusing to put my knowledge to practical use because I was scared."

Jackson wanted to laugh. The only thing he'd ever seen Loralei Lancaster afraid of was the water. And not even that was actually stopping her. Sure, she struggled with it, but she had walked onto the *Emily*'s deck despite the fact that it had terrified her. She'd refused to let the fear win. That strength and perseverance impressed Jackson.

"What do you mean?"

"I was so damn determined not to turn out like my parents, who were filled with a burning need to find, search and discover. While I was sitting inside some stuffy library I could pretend that my drive wasn't anything like theirs. That I wasn't ever going to choose my career over family and friends. I could fool myself into believing my love for history, for digging and exploring hadn't come from either of them because my skin wasn't tinged red by the sun and my body wasn't dripping wet from the water."

She moved, fitfully, with no purpose except to expel some of the uneasy energy racing around inside her. Jackson understood. That energy was often what drove men crazy in the field when one movement could mean making yourself a target, but one more second standing still could mean losing your ever-loving mind.

"The *Chimera*… At first I wanted to ignore her. My plan was to file the information away and just forget I'd ever found it. Because searching for treasure wasn't something a true scholar should do. But then I realized just how desperate Lancaster Diving had gotten and I didn't have much choice. She's the answer to our financial problems and the only way I can save the company my dad poured every ounce of his being into."

She laughed, the exhalation of sound far from happy. "You'd think I'd want to see it fail. And maybe a small part of me does. I mean, he spent a hell of a lot more time on that broken ship out there than he ever did with me."

Jackson had already known some of what she'd just shared. But it was somehow comforting having her give him that insight voluntarily. He shouldn't want to get to know her. None of this should matter. But it did.

When he'd first learned who Loralei was, she'd simply been the daughter of the man who'd stolen from him. But over the past few days Loralei had become real to him. He'd seen her fear, watched her determination and even now saw the swirl of frustration and hope and residual pain in her eyes.

He respected her, even if he didn't particularly want to.

Maybe she wasn't using him or lying to him. Maybe this wasn't some elaborate ploy to screw him over in the end, as he'd feared. Maybe what was happening between them meant more than he'd initially thought.

"I told myself that was all finding the *Chimera* was. A way to save the company, nothing more. But the minute that cannon surfaced…I knew I'd been lying to myself. I have it. That compulsion I saw glimmering deep inside my mother's eyes right before she left me that last time. The same drive that kept my father away for months at a time."

He could hear the mingled awe and anguish in her voice. The conflicting emotions made his own chest tighten and ache.

"I grew up thinking their obsession with diving on wrecks was like an illness. My mom would put me to bed, not with fairy tales, but stories of pirate ships and hurricanes and lost treasure. I loved those stories, until she wasn't there to tell them anymore. And then I hated them. But after yesterday…"

That ingrained fascination was a piece of herself Loralei hadn't wanted to admit to. Or like.

That reluctant need was something he could identify with. How many times had he wished he could claim his stepmom as his real mother? But she wasn't. Oh, she'd made him feel wanted and loved. But even that wasn't enough to counter the knowledge that his real mom, the one who'd given birth to him, had walked away without so much as a backward glance.

And no amount of wishing the situation were different or willing his own emotions about it away could change that truth.

He was so caught up in his own twisted memories that it took him several moments to realize Loralei's body was trembling. The awareness blasted through him, sharp and uncomfortable because he wanted to help her, but had no idea how.

Smoothing his palm down the center of her body, he spread his fingers across her tummy. The curve of his thumb brushed the underside of her breast and his pinky stroked the skin above her navel.

Needing to fill the charged silence, he asked, "What do you love about history?"

He wanted to know, but he also thought maybe it was something they could share—did share.

Loralei dragged in a deep breath, her ribs expanding and contracting beneath his hand. She shook her head where she'd buried it under his chin, and her dark hair dragged across his skin, tickling his nose.

"I love learning about people. Trying to figure out what drove their choices. Not just the important people but everyday folks. How did they live? How did they love? Were they really that different from us deep down?"

"I don't think so," Jackson said, because it was something he'd thought about himself as he'd devoted those years to the *Chimera*.

"Human beings are the same no matter the century. We're driven by the need for something—love, money, power, prestige. That *thing* is different for everyone, but we're all looking for something."

She was silent for several seconds, long enough for Jackson to think he'd misunderstood what she was trying to say.

Until she asked, "And what do you need, Jackson Duchane?"

What did he need?

A month ago, hell, a few days ago, his answer would have been swift and unequivocal. "The *Chimera*."

But now, as the words left his mouth, they didn't quite taste right. Oh, he still wanted the ship. But for the first time in years, he wasn't sure finding it would be enough.

He'd devoted every spare moment to solving her puzzle. Going hard as a SEAL, and then going harder whenever he had down time, to uncover those secrets held hostage by history and the beautiful ocean. He'd been driven to uncover the truth locked inside the ship herself. Driven to prove his worth to his grandfather, father, stepmother... and mother.

He'd always been that way. His father, stepmother and sister had always joked the way to get his attention was to hand him a puzzle without an obvious solution. The harder the problem, the more stubborn he'd become at finding the answer.

Relentless, that was how they'd described him.

That trait had served him well in the Teams. Had gotten him through the hellacious training and made him a valuable member to the brothers serving beside him.

Loralei was just as much of a puzzle to him as the *Chimera*. Maybe more of one. Each time he thought he had her figured out, she'd say or do something to convince him he had it all wrong.

Like right now. Until tonight, he never would have labeled her a cuddler, but there she was with her body burrowed tightly against his, her voice raspy with exhaustion and the aftereffects of screaming his name.

At the memories, his cock stirred to life, nestled between them.

Loralei looked up at him and flashed a knowing grin. "Insatiable."

"Only with you." Which was the god's honest truth. He liked sex as much as the next guy, but Loralei was the first woman with whom he could have a mind-blowing orgasm and still crave more.

She just shook her head. "The *Chimera*, huh? That's the easy answer. But assuming I accept it…why is finding her so important to you?"

He wanted to answer her, to reward the vulnerability she'd just shared with some of his own.

"The legend of the *Chimera* has been handed down in my family for generations."

Loralei sucked in a hard breath. It was practically silent, except for a telltale hitch at the very end. But he felt it.

"What…what do you mean?"

Rolling onto his back, Jackson took her with him, tucking her into the warmth of his body and cocooning the covers around them both.

"My name's Jackson."

"Yes," she said, her eyebrows knitting together.

"My sister's name is Kennedy."

"Okay?"

"We're both named for presidents."

"What does that have to do with the *Chimera*? Neither of those presidents was around during the Civil War."

"True, but Jackson's presidency was about 25 years earlier. He was from Tennessee."

"You're not telling me anything I don't already know."

He tugged at a lock of her hair. "Okay, Ms. Historian. One of my ancestors was a distant cousin of Jackson's. He carried on the family tradition of military service, and when the Civil War started he fought for the Confederacy. He didn't stay in the field long though, quickly working his way up the ranks. He was aboard the *Chimera.*"

"Oh, my God," she breathed out.

"Yep. My ancestor went down with the ship. But one of his slaves survived. Or so the legend goes. The only person known to have survived the wreckage, he spent days adrift on a piece of the ship's hull, finally washing ashore on one of the smaller Caribbean islands. But, unfortunately, he couldn't tell anyone exactly where the *Chimera* went down."

"Why can't I find any record of this survivor?"

"Because my family was influential and wealthy. They knew exactly what was in the hold of the *Chimera* and wanted to keep any information about her possible resting place to themselves. However, it didn't do them much good. In the middle of a war, they didn't have the resources to spare for a search."

Loralei studied his face. "So this is personal for you."

"Yes. From the moment I could reason, my grandfather would tell me the story of the *Chimera*. My own personal fairy tale complete with subterfuge, war and gold."

"It isn't about the gold, though."

Jackson laughed. "Oh, it's about the gold."

She waved away his statement. "It isn't. Not really. Sure, you want it—who wouldn't?—but you want to be able to tell your grandfather *you* found her."

"My grandfather is gone."

"That won't prevent you from telling him, will it?"

His mouth twisted into a crooked line. "No." He had every intention of making the graveyard his first stop after they found the *Chimera,* right after calling his father, who would be almost as ecstatic as his grandfather would have been.

"It's history. Your history."

Jackson nodded.

Loralei was quiet for several minutes. He let his fingers play across her warm, smooth skin, making mindless patterns as he waited for whatever she would say or do next.

"I understand why you want her so much, Jackson. But I can't afford to just step aside and let you have her. I need this find. Without it, Lancaster Diving is going under. There are men who depend on us for their living, having worked for my father for years. I owe them this."

Slowly, she buried her face in the hard planes of his chest and whispered, "I'm sorry."

SEVERAL HOURS LATER, Loralei's stomach growled. Loudly.

Behind her, she heard Jackson's soft chuckle. With a grin on her face, she threw her elbow back, enjoying the exaggerated *oomph* that came out of his mouth when he rolled into a ball to protect himself from another attack.

"Ouch, woman."

"Please, that didn't hurt. Your abs are made of steel. I'm more likely to dislocate my elbow than put a dent in your belly."

"My belly isn't the one I'm worried about. I think you're harboring a small animal inside yours. And he's angry. And hungry."

"Someone interrupted my midnight snack." Loralei started to bound out of bed, but Jackson snaked an arm around her waist and had her tumbling back against him.

"Where do you think you're going?"

"To get something sharp and pointy to hurt you with." Loralei couldn't stop a smile from spreading across her face and ruining the tough words. "Or to grab some break-fast."

"Food. Let's go with food."

Lifting her up again, Jackson rolled out of bed and placed her feet on the floor. Somehow, he managed to keep his hands on her the entire time.

She pulled out of his grasp and leaned down to snag her clothes off the floor, not realizing her mistake until it was too late. The crack of his palm against her naked ass resounded through the room.

Loralei jumped and squealed, instinctively rubbing a hand over her rear. It didn't hurt, not really. Warmth spread across her skin, but it was more the surprise of his gesture than anything else that had her reacting.

"What was that for?"

"The elbow… And the drink you dumped over my head the first night we met."

"That was days ago."

Jackson shrugged, his bright blue eyes twinkling. "Much like an elephant, I don't forget."

"Forget? It didn't seem to bother you then. If I remember correctly, you didn't even wipe the drink off your face."

He snagged her around the waist, pulling her tight into his body. Loralei's back arched, not because she wanted away, but in order to press closer.

"That's because I was too busy staring at you."

She liked this easy going Jackson. The comfortable teasing felt right. A pleasant sensation bubbled up inside her chest. Loralei realized she probably should try to quash it, but she didn't want to. Not right now. Reality and all the reasons why this was fleeting would press in soon enough. Was it so wrong to want to enjoy the moment while she could?

Attempting to keep a severe expression, she glared at him. Her lips still twitched at the corners.

She'd get him back.

The ship was still quiet as they entered the galley. Loralei cleaned up the mess they'd left from last night while Jackson whipped up an omelet full of cheese, peppers, spinach and ham.

Grabbing their plates and two cups of coffee, she expected him to steer her to the dining room. Instead, his hand pressed firmly at the small of her back, he maneuvered her up to the top deck.

Everything was quiet, except for the soft swish of water as it slapped rhythmically against the hull of the *Amphitrite*. The sun hung low, creeping over the horizon and illuminating everything with a golden-rose hue. The kind of color that made the world appear magical and perfect.

Weaving between the equipment, he led her to the far side of the ship, careful to settle her facing away from the water. Finding a perch, he leaned against it and settled her next to him.

He handed her the plate, placing her coffee cup onto the deck at her feet. "Mmm," she murmured, unsure if her satisfaction was thanks to the delicious food he'd made or the comfortable sensation of sharing the moment with him. That wasn't something she was used to—and it certainly wasn't something she'd expected to find with him.

They stayed that way for several minutes, eating until Loralei didn't think she could take another bite.

But even then, Jackson didn't move to end the moment. He set the remnants of their meal aside.

His arms tightened around her body. The steady rise and fall of his chest lulled her.

For the first time since he'd walked up to her table at that bar, Loralei began to wonder what would happen when this was all over. When one of them found the *Chimera*. Would they each go their separate way and pretend their tropical interlude had never happened?

She didn't see how to get around it. One of them would win and the other would lose. She didn't think there was any way to recover from that.

A few days ago that thought hadn't bothered her. This morning it definitely did.

That knowledge made her want to pull away from him, to protect herself from the pain that was sure to come her way. But when she tried, Jackson simply tightened his hold. She couldn't fight him, at least not with strength.

"What are you doing, Jackson?"

"Enjoying the cool morning breeze."

"That isn't what I meant."

"I know, but it's the only answer I have for you right now."

And that was less than reassuring. In fact, it somehow made her more anxious. Jackson Duchane was the kind of man who always had a plan. He instinctively knew where he was going and exactly how he was going to get there.

If he was out of his element here, she had no hope in hell of navigating this path without paying a major price.

But when he leaned forward, ran his lips down the column of her throat, Loralei couldn't find the will to push him away.

14

"What do you think you're doing?"

Loralei jumped at the sound of a voice behind her. Suppressing a surge of guilt, she slammed her phone down over the papers she'd been reading.

She'd tried to forget the photographs were on there, but they'd been calling to her all morning, begging her to take another look. To seriously study.

There was one in particular, a screen shot of a historical document that had been niggling at the back of her brain. She didn't quite understand the significance and how it was tied to what had happened to the *Chimera*.

Unable to stand it any longer, she'd decided to text a copy of the picture to a friend at the university. Although the moment her phone had made the whooshing sound to let her know the message had been sent her stomach had begun to churn with guilt.

Which only increased the erratic thumping of her heart until she realized the angry voice belonged to Brian and not Jackson.

When the rest of the ship had started to stir, Jackson had gone to check in with Marcus. Left to her own devices,

Loralei had decided to pull out her research and pick up where she'd left off.

The ease of their early morning had disappeared thanks to the uncomfortable surge of her guilt.

"What are you talking about?" she asked, her palm beginning to sweat where it hid her secret. Not that she thought Brian would care particularly, but she did.

Her conscience told her she should forget she had the photos, but the scholar inside had colluded with the devil on her shoulder saying that Jackson's information might help her uncover something important.

Grasping her arm, Brian pulled her around to face him. Her back connected with the wall. Her gaze stayed glued to the phone left on the table a few feet away. At least it was face down. And hopefully her locked screen would kick on in a few seconds.

Brian crowded into Loralei's personal space, blocking out most of the small room.

"Your dad would be furious if he knew you'd screwed Jackson Duchane's brains out last night."

That got her attention. She dragged her focus back to the man in front of her. "How—"

Brian spoke right over her. "He's been stealing our clients for months, Loralei. Your father fired him. And you jumped into his damn bed…let him into your body."

His mouth curled with disgust. His eyes flashed as they scoured her up and down, as if she was suddenly covered in filth.

Unease skittered beneath Loralei's skin. It made her angry—at herself and Brian. "It's none of your business who I sleep with."

"It is when you're allowing your libido to overrule your brain and putting this salvage in jeopardy. Wake up, Loralei. He's just using you."

Dread curled through her belly, making her skin tight and uncomfortable. Unwittingly, Brian had given voice to the tiny kernel of doubt she'd been trying to pretend didn't exist. Why was Jackson spending so much time with her? Helping her crew? Was it really because he was a good guy—which was what her heart was telling her—or because he was maneuvering her…and getting great sex out of the situation to boot?

She gave voice to the same arguments she'd been using inside her own head. "How is he using me, Brian? Our team found the cannon."

"And you told him all about it."

How did Brian know that? The unease creeping across her skin ballooned into full-fledged alarm. For the first time she realized they were alone in the small space. The only thing that kept her from total panic was the realization that several men probably occupied the rooms close by and would hear her scream if she absolutely had to.

But she didn't want to.

Because Brian had been with her father forever. She'd known him most of her life. Hopefully, she was overreacting here. Letting her own heightened awareness and guilt breed something that wasn't truly there.

"What was the harm? He'll know soon enough when we publicize the find. It was professional courtesy."

"It was pillow talk."

Rearing back, Brian let his hand fly, smacking it against the wall beside her head. Loralei cringed away from the impact, even if it was nothing more than a reverberation. He hadn't intended to hit her. She knew that. But that didn't stop the gasp of surprise from slipping through her parted lips.

Brian's eyes widened. His gaze chased from the point

his hand pressed against the wall to her startled, frightened expression.

"Loralei, I'm…I'm sorry. I didn't mean…"

He dropped his head, his forehead coming to rest against the wall beside her. He was close, close enough that she could feel his breath fluttering against her skin.

How could the same sensation from Jackson send her blood racing while having Brian this close made her skin cold and clammy?

She stood perfectly still, uncomfortably trapped and afraid of what a single movement might cause.

"I just don't want to see you make a mistake you'll regret. Your father worked hard for this. He had dreams of leaving you the legacy of the *Chimera*. He knew he wasn't a great father, but hoped providing some security for you would make all the sacrifices you were forced to endure growing up worth it. He hated Duchane. Would hate knowing that you've chosen him."

Slowly, Brian pushed away. His arms stiffened, putting a foot of space between them, although it didn't much alleviate the uneasy feeling filling her.

Then he raised his eyes, tortured and sad, to hers and said, "Especially when there's another choice," before walking away.

She stood there, trembling, hands clasped beneath her chin in an effort to stop the motion. Her body sagged against the wall. Thank God it was there to hold her up.

Brian's words echoed through her head. They were words she'd wanted to hear all of her life. That her father had given a damn about her and understood exactly what his choices had done to her.

But hearing them now wasn't enough. Because they hadn't come from her dad.

The *Chimera* was screwing with her brain. Pulling her

in too many different directions. She desperately wanted
to find the ship. Not just for her father, but for herself.

Brian was right about one thing. Being with Jackson
complicated things.

But not enough for her to walk away. Not now.

Not yet.

JACKSON WAS RESTLESS, and not just because his own search
for the *Chimera* had ground to a halt. No one could do
anything while they waited for the tugboat to arrive and
retrieve the injured *Emily*.

Gripping the curved edges of his phone, Jackson said,
"No, I don't need you out here right now, Knox." Hadn't
he said the same exact words to his other partner only a
few days ago? He appreciated their enthusiasm for this
project, but finding the *Chimera* was his baby.

"Then what the hell is going on?" Knox asked. "Marcus
said the whole team is sitting on their thumbs."

He was going to have a nice chat with Marcus.

"The *Chimera* is my assignment. I know how to run
my own goddamn ship."

"Apparently not. You're wasting time and money, Jack.
Trident is solid at the moment, but searching for the *Chimera* isn't cheap."

Jackson knew that. He'd been a major part of all the
work that had gone into raising the capital to fund this
mission.

"What would you have me do, Knox? Her ship was in
danger of sinking. You think I should have watched them
go down? Or maybe I should just dump them into their
lifeboats and sail away without a second thought."

There was a long pause on the other end of the line.
Jackson could just envision Knox. The other man was
known for his laid-back, life-of-the-party attitude. But

Jackson knew better. He was fully aware that the facade was intentional and hid the battle-toughened heart of a fourth-generation soldier.

"Of course not," he said, irritation swamping his voice. "No one's saying that. But this woman... I'm worried about her influence over you."

Jackson bit back a growl. "You shouldn't be."

"Loralei Lancaster isn't a friend, Jackson."

"I'm fully aware of that."

Another long pause suggested Knox didn't believe him. Jackson wasn't sure he believed himself anymore.

"The tug should be here soon. We'll get back on track. And I'm close. I can feel her, Knox. I know she's just waiting for us to find her."

"I hope so, Jack. It would suck if Lancaster beat us to her after everything we've put into finding the wreck."

Knox wasn't wrong.

And maybe as much as he hated the conversation, it was what Jackson needed to get his head back in the game.

So, for the next several hours Jackson tried to forget Loralei was on the *Amphitrite*. But it was difficult, and that bothered him on several levels. He was used to being in control—of himself and the situation around him. It was clear he had almost none right now.

Over the years Jackson had had his fair share of short-term flings. Not once in that time had he ever wanted more than what he'd had—days, weeks, on occasion months. Whenever it was over, he'd walked away without a second thought.

He was beginning to worry that walking away from Loralei would be different. Maybe impossible.

And that was a problem, because this couldn't continue. Logically, he realized they had no future. There was a slim chance they might make it through the current situation without hating each other. But she would never want a life at sea, and he couldn't imagine her waiting at home for him to drop by now and then—she'd had enough of that with her father.

Pushing up from the chair he'd settled into, Jackson prowled out of the room. Maybe he'd just go grab a beer from the fridge. But as he passed a room several doors down, he couldn't help but look inside. And what he saw caught his attention.

His own goddamn research was spread out across the table. Current maps, a rendered drawing of the *Chimera*, cargo lists, passenger manifest. He stepped inside, looking closer. Hell, even his notes were there.

He couldn't decide if he was impressed Loralei had the guts to be so blatant or ready to throttle her. Maybe both. Anger and disbelief surged through him, but he made a valiant effort at checking them.

Looking closer, he realized at some point Loralei must have taken his work and added to it.

But before he could get a good look he heard a noise in the corridor. He had no idea why his first instinct was to hide. Maybe too many years working top-secret missions. It wasn't as if she'd tried to conceal any of this stuff. It was spread out on his own ship.

That still didn't stop him from heading back into the hallway as quickly as possible.

Loralei walked out of the galley, a mischievous grin on her face. An apron covered her tank top and tiny shorts, its ruffles skimming the tops of her bare thighs.

"Where did you get that thing?" he asked. It was hot pink for heaven's sake.

She shrugged. "Apparently it was a gag one of your guys brought on board to torture someone on the team."

How did he not know about this? "I don't think I want to hear that story."

Especially not when she looked delicious in it and he was currently harboring fantasies of her wearing nothing but it later.

And this was the problem. The minute she was close, every other need, fear or want flew out the window, and all he could think about was her. Not just sex, although he'd take as much of that as possible. But *her*.

Watching her laugh. Seeing the way her nose crinkled when she was upset or concentrating. The way, even in the face of her fear, she'd stood up in that boat so she could count her team and make sure everyone was okay.

Dammit, Knox was right. He was in serious trouble.

Loralei tossed him a saucy smile and crooked her finger at him. He was powerless to do anything but close the gap between them. Jackson didn't stop until his arms were around her and she was sighing against his mouth.

His eyes slid shut, allowing him to sink into the sensation of the kiss. Heat bubbled through his blood.

"You smell like rosemary and garlic," he murmured, pulling away.

"I hope you like Italian. It isn't much, what with supplies being limited."

He put a finger against her lips, silencing her words. "I'm sure it'll be amazing. Thank you for cooking."

"It was the least I could do considering you've taken in my crew." Her lips tipped upward. And suddenly Jackson wasn't hungry at all. At least not for anything but her. If he had his way, he'd pick her up and take her back to his room. But she'd spent so much time that he refused to let it go to waste. Stepping out of her embrace, he put some space between them. But he slid his hand down her arm until their fingers twined together. "Lead the way."

She turned, giving him a delectable view of her ass, barely covered by the jagged edge of her torn jean shorts. Unable to stop himself, Jackson reached out and cupped her rear, letting his fingers slide beneath the fabric around her thigh.

Loralei jumped and smacked a hand down over his roaming fingers, tossing a warning glare over her shoulder.

"Behave. We're not eating alone."

His entire world deflated. He'd had visions of *Lady and the Tramp* moments where he got to feed her bites of pasta and lick sauce off her mouth.

They walked into the long dining room where both crews were already crowded around the tables. The air smelled amazing—tomatoes, onions, garlic and spices— almost as good as Loralei.

Several of the men from her team sent him assessing stares.

From across the room someone yelled, "You've done it now, Loralei. We all know you can cook. You'll never get out of galley duty again."

She laughed, her head dropping back as her eyes twinkled. "That's what you think, boys."

"Did you try her oatmeal raisin cookies?"

"To die for!"

"I didn't get any," Jackson murmured into her ear.

"You got something better," she whispered.

The tension that had filled their first meal together had disappeared. The teams mingled together tonight. Everyone joined in the banter. Everyone except Brian. Tucked into a dark corner at a far table, the other man didn't bother to hide his displeasure.

Not that Jackson gave a damn. He wasn't particularly enamored with the man himself. Turning away from Brian's glare, he concentrated on Loralei.

She dished out a plate, passing it to him before filling one for herself. He watched Loralei interact with the guys from both teams, treating everyone equally.

What surprised him, but probably shouldn't have, was that somehow Loralei had managed to fit right in. She'd become like everyone's little sister. In a way, it reminded him of Kennedy and the guys she worked hard to keep in line whenever they were in port.

The men ribbed Loralei. He loved the way her honey-toned skin flushed warm when the conversation verged on inappropriate. And the guys weren't above dishing out some veiled zingers, specifically about the two of them.

As they all settled in, everyone relaxed and began to accept the unusual situation, forgetting they were rivals fighting for the same treasure.

Jackson scooted closer to Loralei, placing his hand at the small of her back as he leaned over to speak to the guy on her other side.

She didn't stop her conversation with Spike, the guy with the scraggly beard sitting across from her. He had to be fifty if he was a day, and the twinkle in his eyes told Jackson he had plenty of experience with trouble. What had a hard band tightening his chest was the way Loralei leaned into his body as she spoke to the other man.

The gesture seemed instinctive, and because of that somehow it meant a hell of a lot more.

He wanted that easiness. Had seen it between his father and stepmother, but never thought to find it for himself. Partly because he'd never bothered to stay with a woman long enough for them to become comfortable together.

What floored him was how quickly it had come on with Loralei. He'd assumed that kind of thing took months and years to develop…not mere days. Especially not in the midst of everything they'd been fighting and experiencing.

Or maybe that was why it had come on so quickly. Maybe saving her life had bonded them in an unexpected way. Loralei certainly wasn't the first person he'd saved— although, she was a hell of a lot softer and more beautiful than the soldiers he'd rescued.

Tossing him a soft smile, Loralei pushed up from the bench, throwing one leg over and then the other. He moved to follow her, but her hands on his shoulders pressed him back down.

"Stay. I'll be right back."

She disappeared through the closed door leading from the dining room into the galley. Even after the door closed, Jackson continued to stare at it, waiting for the moment she'd return.

Which was probably why he didn't notice Brian's approach until the man was standing behind him.

All around them, the men went silent. That more than anything clued Jackson in to what was happening.

His body tightened, instinct kicking in a little late to the party. Damn, he'd been out of the Teams too long if a man like Brian could walk up to him without notice.

He needed to get back to the gym and kick Asher's ass for a refresher course.

"What do you think you're doing?" Brian asked from behind him.

Jackson spun on the bench to face the other man, but kept his seat. "Having dinner," he responded with a negligent shrug.

Brian stared at him out of hard, flat eyes. The guy was angry and spoiling for a fight.

Damn. Loralei was going to be upset no matter how this ended.

But his ego and integrity wouldn't allow him to sit still

and let the other man pound on him—verbally or physically.

"With her. What do you think you're doing with Loralei?"

Jackson let a single eyebrow crook up. "Having dinner."

Brian growled low in his throat. He wrapped his fists into Jackson's shirt and yanked, trying to pull him to his feet. Jackson let him, keeping his own hands at his sides. For now.

Brian was out of his element, although that seemed to be the norm for the other man. He liked to talk and walk big, but didn't have the skills or balls to back up the bluster. Which, in Jackson's opinion, was how he'd gotten into trouble with the explosive charge months ago.

"She isn't a plaything, you asshole. She just lost her father. She's alone and vulnerable, and you're taking advantage of that."

He was doing no such thing. "No, she isn't a plaything," Jackson said. "She's a beautiful woman who can take care of herself. She knows what—and who—she wants…and doesn't want."

Brian's eyes flashed fire. Apparently not the brightest thing to say if he'd hoped to defuse the situation. But his gut told him that wasn't going to happen anyway, so…

"Give her some damn credit, man. She's not a little girl."

"I'm well aware of that."

"I bet you are," Jackson said.

"Fuck you, man."

"No thanks," Jackson taunted, a smile curling his lips. "You're not my type."

Jackson ducked the first punch. Brian might as well have taken out a billboard he'd telegraphed his intentions so damn loud. And Jackson had never been the kind of man to stand still and give anyone a free shot, especially when they didn't deserve it.

Around them, several of the men jumped out of their seats. The back of his neck started tingling with warning. There were plenty of guys here who might take Brian's side. And he had no doubt his own crew would back him up. That was exactly what he didn't need, an all-out brawl between both crews.

As much as it went against his nature, Jackson clenched his hands into fists and kept them by his sides. Giving in to what Brian wanted would feel good, but it wouldn't be the smartest move right now—not for him or Loralei.

Brian didn't seem to think that far. He drew his arm back and let another punch fly. Jackson ducked, grabbed Brian's fist and used the man's momentum to send him stumbling several steps away.

That did nothing to cool Brian's anger. In fact, it made his skin flare red with unchecked fury.

Jackson began bouncing on his feet, preparing for Brian's next move. The man swung and missed, his fists flailing with temper more than skill. Unfortunately, even a blind squirrel uncovered a nut now and then, and Brian managed to land a few shots—one to Jackson's face, another couple to his body.

What he wasn't ready for were the words that poured out of Brian's mouth as he moved. Or his own reaction to them.

"She's using you, Duchane. Spreading her legs just to get closer to the gold. It's all she cares about. Her dad's legacy. You're nothing but a tool."

Brian's lips twisted into a self-righteous smirk. "She'll get exactly what she wants and when she's done with you, she'll head straight back to the perfect life she's built for herself in Chicago."

Jackson's body flooded with heat. Stepping into Brian, he twisted his hand in the other man's shirt, pulled his face close.

"What did you say?"

"You heard me."

"I heard you imply that Loralei's no better than a gold-digging whore," he growled.

It was one thing for Brian to take cheap jabs at him, but entirely another for him to disparage Loralei's reputation.

Hauling back, Jackson put every ounce of power he had behind the punch. It landed squarely on target, right beneath Brian's chin, sending the other man sprawling backward. His arms windmilled. His body hit one of the tables before ricocheting off the hard edge and collapsing to the floor in an uncoordinated heap.

A clatter sounded behind him. Silverware and plates hitting the floor and breaking.

15

"WHAT THE HELL is going on?" Loralei's raised voice shot into the room.

She rushed straight past him, skidding to her knees beside Brian, tossing Jackson a glare on her way by.

"Are you okay?" she asked, pulling Brian's shoulders up off the floor and cradling his head in her lap.

Brian nodded, giving her a glazed look that Jackson had to admit made him pretty damn proud. One solid right hook and the man was dazed and confused.

"Infantile children. I can't leave you alone for five minutes." Waving at one of the other men from her crew to help her, Loralei ushered Brian to his feet.

He swayed slightly, leaning heavily against Loralei's shoulder.

Jackson didn't particularly want to help Brian, but he sure as hell didn't want the man draped around her, either. Stepping forward, he tried to take Brian's weight, but Loralei pushed him away.

"You've done enough."

Jackson ground his teeth together, trying to find a lid to push back down over his temper. "Enough? What's that supposed to mean?"

"You knocked him on his ass, Jackson. With one punch. You're a SEAL, for God's sake, and have at least forty pounds of solid muscle on him. Brian isn't anywhere near your weight class."

"Which is why I ignored his jabs and insults…until he suggested you were exchanging sex for information."

Loralei gasped.

The room went utterly silent.

Her skin flushed bright red and Jackson immediately regretted his words. Not because she didn't deserve to know, but because he could have found a more private way to explain what had happened.

His temper had gotten the better of him, something that rarely happened.

"What is he talking about?" she asked Brian, switching her glare to the other man. Jackson had to admit that made him feel slightly better.

Brian, his intelligence finally returning, kept his mouth shut. But one of Jackson's crew didn't have any problem piping up.

"Jackson's right. He tried to ignore the asshole. Took a couple hits himself without returning fire, too."

Just the mention of those punches had his jaw throbbing and the tiny cut on his mouth aching.

Loralei's gaze bounced between the two men, clearly uncertain who to trust. Jackson didn't say anything more. Was it wrong to want her to believe he was a decent guy? The kind who wouldn't throw a punch like that without good reason?

Something dangerous settled inside him when she reached for Brian's arm draped around her shoulder and removed it. Another guy from her crew moved in, taking her spot and helping Brian shuffle out of the galley.

Loralei grabbed Jackson's hand and marched through

the throng of men standing by, eagerly watching the drama unfold. She led him out of the room, and he let her, wondering just what she planned to do with him. It was clear from her heavy steps that her temper was still simmering fairly close to the surface.

She wound through the ship toward his stateroom, not stopping until they were both crammed into the tiny attached bathroom.

Swinging around, she tugged on his shirt until his knees folded beneath him and his butt landed on the closed toilet lid. Loralei was still glaring as she turned to a cabinet, snagged a clean cloth and started running water in the sink to wet it.

With sure movements, she reached for the hem of his shirt and yanked it up over his head. He bit back a hiss when cotton scraped against his abraded skin, sending a shock of pain through his system.

Curling a hand over her hip, Jackson pulled her into the open V of his thighs.

"Don't," she said, the single word still stiff and unhappy.

He leaned forward, letting the crown of his head rest against her belly.

She sighed, a deep exhalation that he felt flutter across his hair. "Dammit," she whispered beneath her breath. But her body relaxed. The tension leaked from her right along with the air.

Bracketing her hands around his face, she applied gentle pressure until he looked up at her.

She shook her head, one corner of her mouth dipping down with exasperation. Her thumb brushed just beside the cut he could feel on his bottom lip.

"You're a mess."

He grinned. "You should see the other guy."

Humor and irritation tinged her gaze. "That isn't funny. What am I going to do with you?"

A wicked, hopeful grin bloomed. "Kiss it and make it better?"

"You're not in any shape for that, ace."

"Wanna bet?"

"Why is it that men think sex can fix everything?"

"Because sex is always a good idea. No matter what. Even if we were dying, at least we'd go out riding a wave of pleasure."

"Like I said, idiots."

Taking the washcloth, she started dabbing at the cut. His jaw throbbed like a son of a bitch, and it actually hurt worse whenever she touched him, but there was no way he was going to tell her that.

His arm was tight around her waist. She was standing between his open thighs, staring down at him with an intense expression.

It had been a long time since a woman had cared for him this way. Possibly because aside from his stepmom and sister, he'd never let anyone get close enough.

Something warm spread through him, starting at his chest and melting out to every one of his extremities. Suddenly the pain he'd been ignoring faded.

She rinsed out the cloth and continued dabbing at his skin. Her fingers and the water were warm. Soothing.

Until that moment he hadn't realized he craved that tenderness. It was addicting, having her soft hands soothing his injured skin.

Jackson let her wash away the blood, sitting still even as his entire body responded. His skin tingled wherever her fingertips touched. The ache behind his fly slowly increased, pushing out the edge of pain coming from the rest of his body.

But this was more than his uncontrolled physical response to her touch. He didn't just want sex. He wanted to worship her body the same way she was soothing his. To take his time and discover everything about her—inside and out.

His cock wasn't the only thing aching, there was a suspicious throbbing sensation right around the center of his chest, as well.

When Loralei was finished with his face, she picked up one of his hands. Staring down at his split knuckles, she breathed out his name before softly brushing her lips across the surface. "I really wish you hadn't done that."

"Defended your honor?"

Loralei's gaze jerked up to his for the first time since she'd hauled him into the tiny bathroom. He realized the gorgeous green was glazed with unshed tears. That alone had him fighting the need to find Brian and beat on him some more—for starting the whole damn thing and making her cry. That wasn't Loralei. She was strong, even taking on the mess her father had left her.

She was so fiercely determined she was willing to face her fear of the water and try to conquer it. Jackson admired that.

Standing up, he kept his arms locked tight around her.

"He wants you, Loralei."

She shook her head, going up on tiptoe, her mouth brushing against his.

It hurt, but he didn't stop her. In fact, he took advantage of the moment, swiping his tongue across the full swell of her bottom lip.

Slowly, she pulled back. "Brian isn't standing in this bathroom with me right now."

"No, no he isn't."

Reaching down, Jackson grasped the hem of her shirt

and pulled it up over her head. Her glorious dark hair fell around her in a soft cloud. Weaving his fingers through it, he swept it back off her face and stood there for several moments, staring down into her intent gaze.

They breathed together. There was something deeper about this moment. A quiet understanding. Warmth spread through his chest as he drank her in.

He wanted to savor her. Take his time and relish every sigh and gasp and hitch of her breath.

TAKING THE FEW strides to the bed, Jackson bent and placed Loralei in the center. Instead of joining her, he stood back, and stared down at her for several seconds.

She fought the urge to cover herself. It was a stupid impulse considering everything they'd shared already, but somehow, the way he was looking at her, left her feeling exposed and vulnerable.

Not because she was nearly naked—her bathing suit had left more skin bare than what she still wore.

It was something in his expression. The intensity filling those bright blue eyes scared her, almost as much as the ocean used to. She felt the familiar roll deep in her belly.

Her hands twitched, instinctively moving to do something, but Jackson reached down and stopped her.

Pressing a knee into the bed, he deliberately stripped away each piece of her clothing—shoes, shorts, bra and panties. His hands roamed, touching every part of her that he revealed. Yet, his gaze never wavered from hers. That left her feeling restless.

He wasn't making her uncomfortable, but suddenly she was uncomfortable in her own skin. Without a single word, he was forcing her to admit—at least to herself— that there was something more going on between them than she wanted.

He saw too much. Had from the moment he'd come into that bar and had sat down beside her. No one had ever looked that deeply into her before.

She was used to being ignored, left and forgotten. Not once since he'd walked into her life had Jackson Duchane made her feel that way.

"God, your skin is so soft," he said, his voice filled with a reverence that should have allayed every one of her fears, but only stoked them higher.

What if he didn't like what he saw? What if he discovered what she'd done? What would she do when she lost this and had to go back to being alone?

She'd been perfectly happy in her life, but now she wasn't sure it would ever be enough again. Not without Jackson there.

He wanted her. Thought she was beautiful. That truth shone clearly from his gaze. Not to mention, he'd said as much. But she wanted more. And that scared the hell out of her.

Because she couldn't have it.

Not with him.

Again, she tried to squirm away, from him and herself. To find a sliver of sanity that would help her keep that barrier between what he was making her feel and what she knew she could have.

This was supposed to be easy. The way Jackson was staring at her didn't feel easy. It felt big. Bigger than anything she'd ever experienced before.

The heavy hands on her hips held her in place.

"Don't, Loralei." She heard the rough edge to his voice and realized she wasn't the only one feeling vulnerable at the moment.

And that stilled the agitated energy deep inside her.

It was her turn to look up at him, warmth pouring

through her body like sunlight. "Come here, Jackson," she finally said.

When he moved close enough, she started pulling at his clothes, needing him to be as exposed as she'd felt just moments ago. Not for herself, but for him. There was something liberating about coming through the uncomfortable sensation, sharing it—and a piece of herself—with him.

She was just as deliberate about removing the rest of his clothes. Unzipping his jeans, pushing everything down his hips and revealing the tight, toned body she'd become so familiar with over the past few days.

Rolling up onto her knees, she brought them closer together. One hand on his shoulder, the other at his hip, she pressed Jackson back until he complied, stretching out on the bed as she had.

She stared down at him, letting her gaze travel the length of his body. There was no denying he was gorgeous by anyone's standards. His body was packed with muscle, golden skin stretched across the straining sinews. But she didn't just see a man with a beautiful outside.

Loralei saw what was beneath. What that body meant.

Jackson was the kind of man who believed in strength and honor. He'd fought to protect the country, taking on dangerous tasks knowing that most of the time no one would ever acknowledge the peril he'd faced. Because it was the right thing to do.

Starting at his feet, Loralei worked her way up his body, paying special attention with her lips and hands to every long-healed scar or brand new mark of pain. Most of them were nowhere near an erogenous zone, but that wasn't what the moment was about.

This was her way of saying thanks for caring about her, for taking in her crew, for being the man he was.

She licked at the discolored skin of a scar at his hip, at

a jagged pucker of tissue that looked suspiciously like a bullet hole near his left shoulder. Kissing his right knuckles, she couldn't stop herself from sucking a single finger deep into the recesses of her mouth.

Jackson pulled in a hard breath and then took the opportunity to stroke his fingertip across her tongue. She felt the caress deep inside, as if he'd been stroking her.

His fingers tunneled through her hair, pulling her up until her eyes locked with his. The heat that washed over her was intense, yet somehow soothing at the same time. Familiar.

She wanted to feel him inside her. For the first time she realized just how wet she'd become. Her sex throbbed with the need to be filled, but only by him.

Rising to her knees, Loralei gripped him and brought him to the entrance of her body. And he watched her, his jaw tense as he let her take control, at least for the moment.

Slowly, she slid down onto him, taking him in inch by inch. The sensation of him filling her was glorious. Perfect.

Yet it wasn't enough. Why did she still feel as if something was missing? That there was more and they simply hadn't reached it yet?

Her hips pressed hard against his. Loralei stayed there for several seconds, waiting, relishing the sensation of him deep inside her.

But Jackson wasn't content to take things slowly.

He sat up, wrapped his arms tight around her body. Gripping her hips, he lifted her, running a hand down her thigh until her legs were wrapped around his waist before surging back inside.

The shift in angle had her pulling in a sharp breath. Taking a tight nipple between his lips, Jackson sucked at the same moment his hips bucked beneath her.

She let out a garbled groan, her head dropping back as her arms tightened their hold around his neck.

She had to move. Now.

Rocking her hips, she timed her movements with each of his thrusts. Their bodies slipped together, rubbing in all the right places.

Never in her life had she felt so close to anyone.

Jackson's hands spread across her back, urging her tighter against him. He stared up, his gorgeous blue eyes glazed yet still completely focused on her.

His powerful thighs contracted beneath her. Loralei threaded her fingers deep into his hair, searching for something to hold on to.

The storm was building, not just the orgasm gathering at the base of her spine, but something deeper swirling dangerously close to the center of her soul.

God, with little effort this man could become so important to her.

He could become everything.

Maybe he already had.

Before that scary realization could take hold, it spun away, ripped out of her thoughts by the grip of an orgasm so powerful there was nothing left but it.

Jackson let out a low cry, surging deep before joining her in the release.

Panting, they clung together, their skin slick. Jackson's face was buried in her neck. Her cheek rested on the crown of his head.

She never wanted to move.

16

HE DIDN'T WANT to leave Loralei. It would be so easy to get used to waking up beside her.

He watched her sleep for a bit, trying to reconcile the past few days.

She wasn't what he'd expected, but he'd known that from the moment he met her. Although that hadn't stopped him from trying to define her by her father's actions.

It would have been so much easier if things had been black and white…if he could blame her for what her father had done.

But there was more to Loralei. More to the situation.

And, damn, he was torn.

He wanted to trust her. To believe that what they'd shared last night had meant as much to her as it had to him.

But that leap of faith was a hard one to take. Especially for a man who'd been disappointed and was used to protecting himself at all costs.

Brian's words rang through his ears once again. "She's using you. She'll be gone as soon as she gets what she wants."

Really, that was his biggest fear. He'd watched his father deal with the devastation of being left. He'd felt the same pain himself, as a child, and never wanted to experience it again.

Not even having a front-row seat to his father and stepmother falling in love and making a life together could erase those harsh lessons.

By dating women who only wanted a physical relationship, he'd avoided risking his heart.

He was starting to think Loralei would be worth risking everything.

But it was early days. He'd met her less than a week ago.

Even as something deep inside was telling him to trust his gut and take the leap, his brain was asking what would happen when one of them found the *Chimera*?

He didn't know the answer. And that scared the shit out of him.

The single thing that had consumed his life for the past decade could conceivably take away any hope of a future with the woman lying next to him.

He didn't want to give up either of them—Loralei or the *Chimera*.

Surely there was a way to have both. He simply hadn't figured it out yet.

Unable to stay still any longer, but unwilling to wake Loralei, Jackson crawled from the bed.

He was in the middle of throwing on some clothes when a soft sound chimed through the room. Jackson walked over to the dresser, intending to silence Loralei's phone so it wouldn't wake her.

But when he saw the screen, he froze.

A text preview lit up the locked screen of her phone. The message was accompanied by a screenshot of a document currently locked inside a safe at his apartment. Of course, a copy sat on his laptop.

According to this document, the *Chimera* was actually owned by a conglomerate of plantation owners with property scattered across the Caribbean—the modern islands of Turks and Caicos, St. John's, the Bahamas. The official paperwork was apparently lost at some point. This appears to be a private copy held by one of those plantation owners. Yes, along with the other information you sent, I'd say your supposition that the *Chimera* could be located off the coast of Rum Cay might be correct.

Anger bubbled beneath his skin like poison. He felt it eating away at him, but couldn't stop the spread of it through his guts, muscles and brain.

Brian had been right.

The only way Loralei could have obtained this document was by snooping through the information on his computer.

When the hell had she done it? From the moment they'd come on board he'd been careful not to leave the machine unlocked…except for the night he'd thought her asleep. Marcus had said he needed to talk for a few minutes so he'd walked up on deck and left his laptop running. Dammit! He knew better, but had gotten complacent.

Jackson let out a few choice curse words.

He turned, stared at the woman sleeping peacefully in his bed. Her dark hair was spread out across his pillow. Her face buried beneath the sheets.

He wanted to hurt her just as much as the pain currently searing through his chest hurt him.

Not physically. He wasn't that kind of man.

For the second time in his life he tasted the bitterness of being used and cast aside. Because that's what she'd planned, right? To get what she needed, by any means necessary, and then leave.

But Jackson wasn't a child anymore, and he had no intention of letting this woman walk away unscathed.

Gripping her phone in his hand, Jackson rounded the bed. He wasn't gentle when he woke her, jerking back the covers and sticking the phone in her face.

"What the hell is this?"

A LOW GROWL started Loralei awake. She heard the words, but it took several minutes for her brain to process them.

"What is what?" she croaked.

Jackson's voice, heavy with anger, registered long before the words on the screen he'd shoved into her face.

That was her phone.

With a text message on the screen.

From her friend Deborah.

She'd sent the screenshot yesterday.

Everything kicked in at once and Loralei's body shot straight up. Her gaze collided with Jackson's blazing blue eyes.

He was irate.

"I..." She tried to read the text. Exactly how much did he know? But before she could pull in more than a few words he was yanking the thing away again.

"Why do you have a copy of a document I own? One I made damn sure was secure with only one copy residing on my hard drive."

Loralei licked her lips. Guilt had made them dry. "It was up on your laptop."

"So you thought you'd take a picture of it and send it to a friend for analysis?"

She went to stand up only to realize that beneath the puddled sheets she was naked. This was not a conversation she wanted to have in the nude.

But she also didn't want to cower on the bed while Jackson stared down at her like some angry Greek god.

Grasping the edges of the sheet, she yanked, wrapping it around her body as she rose.

"I didn't go into that room intending to snoop, Jackson."

"So you had good intentions for wandering into my office in the middle of the night while everyone thought you were asleep?"

She'd been startled awake and swamped by guilt, but now her own temper was making an appearance.

"Yes, I did. And I resent that you'd imply otherwise."

Jackson flashed her phone screen. "This suggests I have every right to imply whatever the hell I want. What part of this did you think was okay, Loralei?"

"What part of invading my privacy by looking at my phone did *you* think was okay, Jackson?"

Jackson's eyes glittered, narrowing to tiny, dangerous slits. But Loralei was too upset to notice the warning he was giving her. Not that she would have heeded it even if she had.

"You really are just like your father, aren't you?" he growled. "Did you sabotage your ship just so you could gain access to the *Amphitrite*? Was Brian right—did you sleep with me to get your hands on my data?"

His words hurt, lancing through her with piercing accuracy. Was that truly what he thought of her? After she'd opened herself up to him last night, against her better judgment.

She didn't dwell on the pain, though, using anger to push it—and him—away.

She planted her forearm in the middle of his chest and shoved. "Absolutely, ace. Because that's the only thing you're good for."

All she wanted was to get out of here and away from

him before she made a bigger idiot of herself. She'd known this had to end at some point, but knowing it and being prepared were apparently two different things.

Jackson's expression shut down, going completely blank. It was eerie to watch a mask slip over him, hiding everything. Until that moment she hadn't realize just how open he'd actually been with her.

She wasn't looking at Jackson Duchane, treasure hunter and dive master. Now, she was staring at Jackson Duchane, lethal soldier.

"What other information is she talking about?"

"What?"

"Your friend. She said along with the other information you sent. What was it?"

Loralei stared at him, her brain spinning.

"It's the least you owe me, Loralei. You took my information and used it. She mentioned Rum Cay."

She swallowed. Torn between what her conscience was telling her to do and what she knew was right for Lancaster Diving and her crew.

He had the information he needed, although he might not realize it. So what was the harm in elaborating on how she'd found it?

If nothing else, it would assuage her guilt. He wasn't wrong. She had used his research, even if it alone wouldn't have been enough. Separately, they'd found important pieces, but they were useless without each other.

"I took the historical data from the hurricane and plugged it into modern tracking software. It provided a slightly altered path for the storm than the one you'd been using. That, along with the information that the *Chimera* had been purchased by a group of wealthy businessmen, one with a plantation on Rum Cay…"

They'd thought all along the *Chimera* had been off

course, but in reality she possibly had been on a secret mission, which only led credence to the idea there'd been gold onboard when she'd sunk.

Jackson's gaze flickered, but the mask didn't drop.

So now they both had the same information. And as soon as the tug and replacement ship arrived later that day it would be a race to see who could get to the *Chimera* first.

17

THE TUGBOAT FINALLY arrived late that morning, accompanied by the ship Loralei had rented to replace the *Emily*.

It was difficult for Jackson to watch Loralei's crew gather what little they'd brought with them. It was more difficult to stay in the background rather than directing the men who would take the listing ship back to port.

Loralei strode around his ship, purposely ignoring him and the situation that had driven them apart, apparently eager to get away from him as quickly as possible.

It shouldn't have hurt, but it did. She was the one who'd betrayed him. Used him.

Meanwhile, Brian spent the time tossing smirks in his direction.

It didn't help when Jackson discovered the *Emily* didn't have the emergency towing procedure legally required for ships of that size. It was such a small, easy thing that James and Brian could have taken care of, but they hadn't.

There was no excuse for ignoring safety procedures. Jackson clenched his fists, thinking of what other things might have been overlooked on the *Emily*. He was angry with Loralei, but the thought of her being in danger still felt like a punch to his gut.

Jackson watched as the team attached lines and prepared both the *Emily* and the tug for departure. It was a slow, painstaking process. The ship might be stable, but there was still the real potential for something to go wrong. The situation was precarious and would be until the *Emily* was back in port where the damage could be repaired.

She was an older ship, but she was still useful and worth saving.

Words sprung to Jackson's lips when Loralei climbed into a launch headed for the *Emily*. He stopped himself halfway across the deck, ready to yank her out of the boat.

Impulse had him wanting her safely on board his ship and not on her own sloping deck. But he didn't have the right to stop her, not anymore. In that moment, it was difficult to remember how pissed off he was.

She was a grown woman and could handle herself.

Damn, he was messed up. And she'd left him that way.

The moment Loralei's crew departed the *Amphitrite*, Jackson tried to push everything out of his head except what he had to do in order to find the *Chimera*.

Loralei and her crew would have to spend precious time transferring their equipment from the *Emily* to their new ship. Jackson had taken that opportunity to get back on track.

Finding the *Chimera* was what was important. Nothing else.

Certainly not Loralei Lancaster.

Rum Cay, the island Loralei's friend had suggested was the likely resting place for the *Chimera*, was several hours away.

Jackson spent the time checking and rechecking his gear. He ordered everyone on the crew to do the same and ignored their grumbles since maintaining equipment for immediate use was standard operating procedure.

Even as restlessness rode his shoulders, Jackson realized his reaction was unusual. Typically during the long hours waiting for a mission to begin, he was the guy sitting calmly in the corner while Knox paced and Asher engaged in mindless movement.

He tried to convince himself he was merely excited over being so close to finding the *Chimera*. But he knew it was so much more, and Loralei was at the center of his unease.

When they finally arrived, he didn't waste any time ordering his team into the water. They had a slight lead and he wanted to take advantage of it.

Donning his gear and getting the team together helped him focus, but the moment he was beneath the water… all bets were off.

The peaceful quiet pressed in. Normally, it was what he liked best about diving, the chance to clear his head and simply be. But that didn't quite work today.

Marcus tapped him on the shoulder to get his attention. Until that moment, Jackson hadn't been aware that he'd been staring off into the distance. Shaking his head, he refocused.

He and his team spent the next hour searching for any sign of the *Chimera*. The divers worked together, covering as much ground as possible in a standard grid pattern as they moved across the sea floor.

A flutter of motion in the distance caught Jackson's eye. One of his guys was waving frantically, swimming furiously to get his attention.

Excitement bubbled up inside his chest as Rick pointed in the direction of an outcropping of rocks about fifty feet away. They'd been avoiding the area because sonar had indicated a major drop-off and the team wasn't prepared to take on those depths today. Especially not without exploring the rest of the surrounding area first.

Following behind Marcus, Jackson headed toward the drop-off, glancing at his equipment to check his air supply. Another forty minutes or so and they'd all need to head up for a break and to change out tanks.

Jackson was mentally shuffling the team, rotating some of the less experienced divers onto the ship and moving the handful of guys he'd left on deck into the water when he rounded the outcropping and nearly slammed into Rick.

Right in front of him sat the most beautiful sight he'd ever seen. What had to be the *Chimera*.

The entire wreck was murky, the water slightly cloudy and dim, most sunlight blocked by the rocky outcropping.

About ten yards down, she rested on a ledge, the edge of the ship balanced precariously over a yawning hole.

If Jackson had to guess, he'd say tossed about in the storm, she'd probably hit the rocks that rose up close to the surface and sunk. The huge hole he could see in the hull supported his theory, but he'd have to get a closer look to know for sure if the damage had caused her to sink or if the hole was the result of hitting the sea floor.

Jackson treaded water and stared. His chest tightened.

This moment should have been the best of his life. The culmination of years working hard, fighting for every speck of information and every extra penny to support the search. Generations of Duchanes had listened to the story of the *Chimera*, but he was here, looking at her with his own eyes.

Yet he wasn't elated. Something was missing. No, someone.

He wanted to share this moment with Loralei instead of the men floating around him pounding each other on the back.

But that wasn't an option.

Gritting his teeth around the soft plastic of the regulator, Jackson headed for the *Chimera*. He'd given up everything for her, he at least wanted a closer look. He still had a little time before he had to head back to the surface.

Signaling for several of the men to stay behind, he motioned Marcus forward with him. Cautiously, they approached the ship.

She was gorgeous. Eerie. He couldn't help but feel a shiver run up his spine knowing people had lost their lives right here. This was their resting place, and as much as he wanted to recover what the hurricane had stolen, he wanted to preserve their memory, as well.

The ship was tipped onto its side. Fish swam in and out of the structure, the entire surface covered with barnacles and sea life, crusted over by time, salt and sand.

He wanted a good look at the hold—to know whether or not her belly held a fortune in gold. But he wasn't stupid enough to go that far before checking the structural integrity of the wreck.

Surely a few feet inside wouldn't hurt, though.

He swam through an opening. It was darker, colder in the shadows cast by what was left of the thick wooden hull. The space he'd entered was small. A cabin maybe? He'd need to study the schematics again to know for sure. With the ship tipped on her side, it was difficult to orient himself.

Spinning around, he took in the sea anemones and plant life that clung to the cracks between the boards. A jagged hole had been ripped in one wall. Before or after impact? It was hard to tell since time and sea water had ravaged the splintered edges.

Something glinted off to his left. At first Jackson thought it was only a fish as eager as he was to explore.

But then it came again, a faint beam of light catching on something metal.

Jackson's heart leapt, adrenaline and excitement mingling together.

Kicking out, he headed for whatever had caught his eye, forcing himself through another hole, probably a narrow doorway, and into another room. It was tiny, debris scattered everywhere. He couldn't tell what most of the broken pieces were, covered with grime and corroded by layers of salt water.

Drifting down, he hovered just above the floor, searching through the debris, and nearly yelled out when he uncovered a perfectly formed circle of metal dotted with dull humps that could be gem stones beneath the filth.

Jackson spun around and smacked straight into the far wall of the room. The entire structure shuddered, giving a deep groan that made fear roll through his belly, obliterating the elation.

Without stopping to think, he kicked out for the doorway on the opposite side. When he'd come in the room had seemed miniscule, right now it might as well have been as vast as the Sahara. Silt and sand started raining down from the cracks in the wall, making the water cloudy and obstructing his vision.

The *Chimera* let out another protesting sound, a cracking whine. Something slammed into Jackson's shoulder, knocking him back against the wall. Luckily, it held. But when the pain and dust cleared, he realized several of the beams had collapsed around him, trapping him inside the tiny room.

LORALEI ORDERED THE crew to drop anchor about twenty yards from the *Amphitrite*.

Frustration rode her hard. It had been torture to watch Jackson's team disappear over the horizon knowing they had a head start on her and there was nothing she could do to stop him.

By the time they'd reached the area, she'd built up a healthy head of steam. It was either that or give in to the tears that threatened, and she refused to let Jackson Duchane have that much hold over her emotions.

Or at least she refused to let him see that he had that much influence over her emotions.

She expected to see Jackson's crew performing the normal tasks necessary during a dive. What she didn't anticipate was the all-out flurry of activity or the sense of panic that seemed to permeate every single person.

Jumping into the launch, she headed over to the *Amphitrite* to figure out what was going on, Brian and several of her team beside her. They boarded the *Amphitrite*, no one paying them any attention.

"Get me that extra tank, dammit! And what do we have that could move those beams out of the way?" Marcus grabbed one of the guys by the collar and hollered into his face, "No, not an ax, you idiot, I'd like to get Jackson out alive, not bury him beneath the rubble of the damn ship! The whole thing is unstable. Do you want the rest of it crushing him?"

Dread twisted through Loralei's belly. "What the hell is going on?"

Barely tossing her a glance, Marcus said, "I don't have time to deal with you right now, Ms. Lancaster. I have a crisis."

Loralei ground her teeth together, fighting back the panic and biting off the words that wanted to spew from her mouth. They wouldn't be helpful right now.

"Obviously. What's going on? Where's Jackson? And what can my team do to help?"

"Jackson is trapped inside the *Chimera*. He went in

to investigate and for some reason the whole damn thing shifted."

Loralei felt the attack coming. The clammy cold followed by the rushing wave of hot. The rolling nausea gripped her belly. Her vision swam, grayed out. Jackson was trapped under water. He was going to die. Just like her mother had.

She couldn't breathe. She might as well have been down there with him, air slowly dwindling to nothing. The nightmares she'd had as a child, what her brain had conjured up as her mother's last moments, merged with her current reality.

"Oh, God." Her legs buckled beneath her. Before she could hit the deck, Marcus grabbed her.

"Breathe, Loralei."

She was losing it. She stared into the other man's face, trying desperately to focus.

He should be down there, helping Jackson right now. What was he doing instead? Holding her up.

Not for the first time since her fear had started, Loralei hated it. Hated herself for the weakness. But today, she had to find the strength to deal with it, because Jackson needed every person on the ship—including her—fighting for him.

And she needed him to live. Desperately. Even if they couldn't repair what had been broken between them, he had to survive this.

Jackson was down there, alone and probably frightened…okay, so maybe he was just alone. She couldn't imagine her big, bad SEAL being afraid of anything. And she was up on this deck losing her mind instead of doing something to help.

Pushing away from Marcus, Loralei squared her shoulders. "Okay, what's the plan?"

"We're taking down tanks so he can change out gear. He's already been down a couple hours. Then we're trying to figure out how to wedge the beams out of the way, at least enough for him to squeeze through."

Nodding, Loralei said, "What can my team do?" Jackson trusted Marcus, so she'd trust his plan and judgment, too.

"We need every man we can get."

Turning back to Brian, Loralei ordered, "Tell everyone to suit up."

Ten minutes later just about every man was in the water. One by one, the group slipped beneath the surface.

And Loralei waited on deck, staring into the deep blue water and trying desperately not to let fear drag her down.

JACKSON CHECKED HIS tank levels one more time. If someone didn't hurry up, he was going to be in serious trouble.

Through the cracks he could just make out Rick on the other side staring in at him. The space might be big enough to pass a regulator back and forth, but he couldn't stay down here forever. And while he knew someone was already in the process of getting another tank, it wasn't like they could get it in to him.

His best bet right now was to force a hole big enough to swim through. If he had to, he could drop his equipment and buddy breathe through the ascent back to the surface.

He and several other guys had already tried to shift the beams, though.

With little left to do but stare at the walls and wait, Jackson's mind spun. The one thing—the one person—he thought about was Loralei.

Regret swamped him. And not because karma was currently paying him a visit.

He shifted the bracelet between his fingers, rubbing

against the smooth metal surface. He wanted to give this to her. To share the find the way she'd shared her excitement over discovering the cannon.

With some distance from his anger and the cold bite of betrayal, Jackson could admit that Loralei was the one who'd finally put all the pieces together and had found the *Chimera*. Without her, he never would have known to send his team to Rum Cay.

Yes, he was still angry she'd snooped through his computer. But faced with the possibility of losing his life, he realized it was worth trying to work through the things that had come between them.

He might not agree with her methods, but he understood how the need to share this with her father and the desperation over Lancaster Diving's financial crisis might have pushed her into doing something she regretted.

Even if she hadn't said the words to him, he'd seen the guilt on her face as she'd confessed to her deception. She hadn't tried to hide the truth from him—at least that was something.

Besides, he wasn't completely innocent. He'd let his own issues cloud his judgment. It wasn't until this moment that he'd understood just what was important. And as much as he'd wanted the *Chimera*, there was something he needed more. The find should be hers. Would be hers. If he ever made it out of this godforsaken wooden box.

A commotion on the other side of the wall caught his attention. A muffled noise. An explosive shiver that sent another cascade of sand and silt floating through the water.

It wasn't coming from where Rick had been, but the adjacent wall. Suddenly, a jagged hole opened up. It got bigger and bigger until a face appeared on the other side. But not one Jackson expected.

What the hell was Brian doing here?

The two men stared at each other through the opening. Although Jackson realized he didn't have the luxury of wasting those precious seconds, he couldn't stop himself. A few moments ago he'd been worried he wasn't going to make it out of the situation alive, and now the man he would have thought most likely to sit and cackle with glee as he watched Jackson die was rescuing him.

Someone pushed Brian out of the way, jolting Jackson back into survival mode.

The hole wasn't big enough for him and his gear to get through. Unstrapping all of his equipment, he shrugged the heavy tanks from his back, but kept hold of them. He needed the weight. Swimming right up to the hole, he stuck his head through and surveyed the cluster of men waiting. Way more than just his team.

Taking a deep breath from his regulator, Jackson dropped everything, pushed his way through the hole and into Marcus's hands. Another regulator was immediately shoved in his direction. Taking the spare tank, he strapped all of the equipment back into place and then, for the first time since the walls collapsed, took a steady breath.

He was going to be fine.

Turning, he looked at the *Chimera*. She just sat there, quiet and contained.

Together, the group headed slowly for the surface. Jackson was used to the painstaking ascent process required after being down so deep, but today it felt like forever before the flat glare of sunlight broke through above him.

He had no idea what to expect. Brian's presence meant Loralei was up there waiting for him. For a moment, a brief one he'd never admit to another living soul, he wondered if maybe he'd been safer trapped inside the *Chimera*.

He wasn't looking forward to this encounter, dealing with the issues that still clouded the air between them. Especially since he didn't know where Loralei's head was. But perhaps telling her that he was planning on giving Lancaster Diving the credit for the find would smooth her temper.

Better to get the coming confrontation over with.

He broke the surface, his gaze automatically scanning up for any sign of Loralei.

She waited, her hands gripped tight around the metal railing, staring at him. The intensity of her gaze ripped straight through him.

Until she collapsed onto the deck, her legs folding under her. Her hands were frozen around the railing high above her, almost as if she couldn't let go.

His only thought at that moment was getting to her.

He hauled himself onto the diving platform. He stripped off equipment, leaving it wherever it dropped as he raced across to her. Water streamed from his body. He didn't care. Not when he slid to a halt on his knees beside her, or gathered her into his arms, getting her all wet.

And she didn't seem to mind, either, clinging to him with a desperation that made his chest ache.

Burying her face in his neck, she whispered, "I thought you were gone."

LORALEI'S MOUTH QUIVERED even as she crushed it against his. She needed to feel him, to know that he was alive and okay.

Pulling back, Jackson smoothed his hands over her face. "I'm fine."

From somewhere deep inside, a sob gushed out. She didn't bother trying to smother it, but let the tears come. Jackson held her, his arms tight, comforting bands around her body, and let the storm of emotions crash over her.

All around them, men surfaced from both teams, climbing back aboard the *Amphitrite* to mill around the deck.

Finally finding control over her voice again, she asked, "What the hell happened?"

"I made a stupid mistake."

Her hands curled into Jackson's arms, slipping across the material of his wetsuit in an effort to find some purchase. "A mistake?"

That was the last thing she needed to hear.

"A mistake is what killed my mother, Jackson. You can't do that, go down there and take unnecessary risks. I can't take it."

An impish grin flashed across his face momentarily before it was gone. "You can't take it?"

"No. Do you know how I felt when they told me you were trapped down there? That they couldn't get you out? Jackson, I need you in my life."

"You aren't pissed at me?"

"Oh, I'm totally pissed at you."

Jackson laughed, the sound rumbling through her body and settling in the center of her chest. It was beautiful.

"That's okay, I'm still pretty angry with you myself. But I have something for you," he said. Shifting his body, he reached behind him and pulled something small out of the bag attached to his waist.

Loralei gasped when sunlight glinted softly off the dulled metal.

Taking her hand, Jackson stretched out her arm before slipping the thing onto her wrist.

She stared down at it, transfixed. Honestly, anyone else probably would have thought it ugly. Covered in gunk, it slid against her skin. To her, it was the most beautiful thing she'd ever seen.

"I found it inside the ship. And the first thing I wanted

to do was give it to you. Loralei, I'm so sorry. We've both made mistakes."

Loralei shook her head. "I don't—"

Laying a finger across her lips, Jackson blocked her mouth and the words she'd been about to say.

"I spent ten years looking for the *Chimera* and you'd devoted less than ten weeks."

"I know," she managed to mumble around his finger.

"But I never would have found the Chimera without your research. You're the one who put all the pieces together."

Unable to stay still any longer, Loralei maneuvered out of Jackson's grasp.

"What I was going to say—" she glared at him "—was that without your research the Lancaster team never would have been searching for the *Chimera*."

Jackson's eyes danced. Grabbing her, he pulled her close and buried his nose in the crook of her neck. "What are we going to do?"

"Know of any good diving companies looking to expand? I have a lot of very skilled men, although I'll admit our ship is a little…injured."

Pulling back, Jackson stared at her. "I'll talk with my partners, but if nothing else, we'll be sharing credit for finding the *Chimera*."

She smiled up at him, her grin so wide it almost hurt. "Does that mean you and I are going to be working together on the recovery?"

"I hope so, but don't you have a job back in Chicago?"

Her grin wobbled. "I do, but…"

"Loralei, I've seen the way your face lights up when you talk about your work. I wouldn't ask you to give that up."

"I don't want to lose that, either, but I don't want to miss out on anything here. I discovered another passion researching the *Chimera*. I'll just have to find a way to have both. Surely there's a university in Florida that might be looking for a history professor."

Jackson laughed, happiness bubbling up in him. Unable to keep the words inside anymore, he pulled her closer and whispered, "I've fallen in love with you. Somehow, along the way, I discovered that the treasure I've spent a huge chunk of my life searching for isn't nearly as important to me as the woman who helped me find it. I want to figure out where this is going."

Jackson waited for her response, his heart pounding fiercely inside his chest. Giving Loralei the power to hurt him took every ounce of courage he had.

This woman could do more damage to him than years of clandestine missions ever could.

Pushing her fingers into the hair at his nape, Loralei tugged until he leaned back and looked her in the eye. "I have no idea when it happened, Jackson, but somewhere in these last few days I've fallen in love with you. The man that you are—honorable, fierce and driven. Don't get me wrong, there are days you make me so frustrated, but you also make me feel safe and wanted, something I haven't always had."

Jackson leaned down and kissed her, pressing their mouths together in a white-hot moment of bliss. He'd never get tired of the sensation that spun through his blood at the taste and touch of her.

Together, they'd found the *Chimera*. Together they'd figure out how to build a life. And remembering all the times she'd fought with him, dumped a drink on his head and battled her own fears, he knew there wouldn't be a single dull moment.

"I never thought I'd say this, but I'm so damn grateful your dad stole my research."

Loralei laughed. "I'm glad he fired your ass."

Jackson growled low in his throat, even as a smile tugged at his lips.

Fate was funny. It had a way of taking a few unrelated events and stringing them together to change your life completely.

And he wouldn't have it any other way.

He'd found the *Chimera*. But more importantly, he'd found the woman he wanted to share the rest of his life with. And that was the greater treasure.

* * * * *

They think they've found the Chimera,
but have they really? Find out with Knox McLemore
and his beautiful nemesis Avery Walsh
in Kira Sinclair's next SEALS OF FORTUNE *title,*
IN TOO DEEP.
Available July 2015.

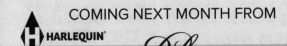
#839 WICKED SECRETS

Uniformly Hot!

by Anne Marsh

When Navy rescue swimmer Tag Johnson commands their one-night stand turn into a fake engagement, former Master Sergeant Mia Brandt doesn't know whether to refuse...or follow orders!

#840 THE MIGHTY QUINNS: ELI

The Mighty Quinns

by Kate Hoffmann

For a reality TV show, Lucy Parker must live in a remote cabin with no help. Search and rescue expert Eli Montgomery tempts Lucy with his wilderness skills—and his body. Accepting jeopardizes her job...and her defenses.

#841 GOOD WITH HIS HANDS

The Wrong Bed

by Tanya Michaels

Danica Yates just wants a hot night with the sexy architect in her building to help her forget her would-be wedding. She's shocked when she finds out she went home with his twin!

#842 DEEP FOCUS

From Every Angle

by Erin McCarthy

Recently dumped and none-too-happy, Melanie Ambrose is stuck at a resort with Hunter Ryan, a bodyguard hired by her ex. Could a sexy fling with this virtual stranger cure her blues?

REQUEST YOUR FREE BOOKS!
2 FREE NOVELS PLUS 2 FREE GIFTS!

♦ HARLEQUIN®

Blaze®

red-hot reads!

YES! Please send me 2 FREE Harlequin® Blaze™ novels and my 2 FREE gifts (gifts are worth about $10). After receiving them, if I don't wish to receive any more books, I can return the shipping statement marked "cancel." If I don't cancel, I will receive 4 brand-new novels every month and be billed just $4.74 per book in the U.S. or $4.96 per book in Canada. That's a savings of at least 14% off the cover price. It's quite a bargain. Shipping and handling is just 50¢ per book in the U.S. and 75¢ per book in Canada.* I understand that accepting the 2 free books and gifts places me under no obligation to buy anything. I can always return a shipment and cancel at any time. Even if I never buy another book, the two free books and gifts are mine to keep forever.

150/350 HDN F4WC

Name _____ (PLEASE PRINT)

Address _____ Apt. #

City _____ State/Prov. _____ Zip/Postal Code

Signature (if under 18, a parent or guardian must sign)

Mail to the **Harlequin® Reader Service:**
IN U.S.A.: P.O. Box 1867, Buffalo, NY 14240-1867
IN CANADA: P.O. Box 609, Fort Erie, Ontario L2A 5X3

Want to try two free books from another line?
Call 1-800-873-8635 or visit www.ReaderService.com.

* Terms and prices subject to change without notice. Prices do not include applicable taxes. Sales tax applicable in N.Y. Canadian residents will be charged applicable taxes. Offer not valid in Quebec. This offer is limited to one order per household. Not valid for current subscribers to Harlequin Blaze books. All orders subject to credit approval. Credit or debit balances in a customer's account(s) may be offset by any other outstanding balance owed by or to the customer. Please allow 4 to 6 weeks for delivery. Offer available while quantities last.

Your Privacy—The Harlequin® Reader Service is committed to protecting your privacy. Our Privacy Policy is available online at www.ReaderService.com or upon request from the Harlequin Reader Service.

We make a portion of our mailing list available to reputable third parties that offer products we believe may interest you. If you prefer that we not exchange your name with third parties, or if you wish to clarify or modify your communication preferences, please visit us at www.ReaderService.com/consumerschoice or write to us at Harlequin Reader Service Preference Service, P.O. Box 9062, Buffalo, NY 14269. Include your complete name and address.

SPECIAL EXCERPT FROM

 HARLEQUIN

Blaze

Military veteran Mia Brandt agrees to a fake engagement to help sexy rescue swimmer Tag Johnson out of a jam. But could their fun, temporary liaison lead to something more?

Read on for a sneak preview at
WICKED SECRETS *by* **Anne Marsh**,
part of our **UNIFORMLY HOT!** *miniseries.*

Sailor boy didn't look up. Not because he didn't notice the other woman's departure—something about the way he held himself warned her he was aware of everyone and everything around him—but because polite clearly wasn't part of his daily repertoire.

Fine. She wasn't all that civilized herself.

The blonde made a face, her ponytail bobbing as she started hoofing it along the beach. "Good luck with that one," she muttered as she passed Mia.

Oookay. Maybe this *was* mission impossible. Still, she'd never failed when she'd been out in the field, and all her gals wanted was intel. She padded into the water, grateful for the cool soaking into her burning soles. The little things mattered so much more now.

"I'm not interested." Sailor boy didn't look up from the motor when she approached, a look of fierce concentration creasing his forehead. Having worked on more than one Apache helicopter during her two tours of duty, she knew the repair work wasn't rocket science.

She also knew the mechanic and…holy hotness.

Mentally, she ran through every curse word she'd learned. Tag Johnson hadn't changed much in five years. He'd acquired a few more fine lines around the corners of his eyes, possibly from laughing. Or from squinting into the sun since rescue swimmers spent plenty of time out at sea. The white scar on his forearm was as new as the lines, but otherwise he was just as gorgeous and every bit as annoying as he'd been the night she'd picked him up at the Star Bar in San Diego. He was also still out of her league, a military bad boy who was strong, silent, deadly…and always headed out the door.

For a brief second, she considered retreating. Unfortunately, the bridal party was watching her intently, clearly hoping she was about to score on their behalf. Disappointing them would be a shame.

"Funny," she drawled. "You could have fooled me."

Tag's head turned slowly toward her. Mia had hoped for drama. Possibly even his butt planting in the ocean from the surprise of her reappearance. No such luck.

"Sergeant Dominatrix," he drawled back.

Don't miss
WICKED SECRETS
by New York Times *bestselling author Anne Marsh,*
available April 2015 wherever
Harlequin® Blaze® *books and ebooks are sold.*

www.Harlequin.com

HARLEQUIN®

A *Romance* FOR EVERY MOOD™

Stay up-to-date on all your romance-reading news with the *Harlequin Shopping Guide*, featuring bestselling authors, exciting new miniseries, books to watch and more!

The newest issue will be delivered right to you with our compliments! There are 4 each year.

Signing up is easy.

EMAIL

ShoppingGuide@Harlequin.ca

WRITE TO US

HARLEQUIN BOOKS
Attention: Customer Service Department
P.O. Box 9057, Buffalo, NY 14269-9057

OR PHONE

1-800-873-8635 in the United States
1-888-343-9777 in Canada

Please allow 4-6 weeks for delivery of the first issue by mail.